MASON

THE PRIDE OF THE DOUBLE DEUCE BOOK 2

KATHI S. BARTON

World Castle Publishing, LLC
Pensacola, Florida
Copyright © Kathi S. Barton 2015
Hardback ISBN: 9781629893228
Print ISBN: 9781629893235
eBook ISBN: 9781629893242
First Edition World Castle Publishing, LLC, August 21, 2015
http://www.worldcastlepublishing.com

Licensing Notes

Cover: Karen Fuller
Editor: Eric Johnston
Editor: Maxine Bringenberg

CHAPTER 1

Mason moved along the fence line looking for breaks. He was out here because he needed to be alone, not because of any report that the fence was down. Instead he had made up a story about the line and needing to check it early this morning, and was enjoying the quiet of the afternoon now. Things at home were...too much, he supposed. He'd never been one to party it up. It wasn't his style to go to bars. Not that he drank at all, but he was a loner and he enjoyed the quiet, like he was finding here on the open area.

When a noise broke his silent reprise, he looked at the big horse coming toward his and frowned. The McBrides were having a hard time of the quiet at their home in the opposite way he was. Three months ago, their son had decided that he didn't want to be a rancher. Their second child, a girl, had moved out long ago for greener pastures. Mason had a feeling that there wasn't much in the way of brother/sisterly love between the two children, but no one had ever confirmed or denied it, so he never asked. Dirk McBride, the son, was an ass anyway, and he'd never met the girl. But he liked Landon and Katie McBride a great deal.

"Mason." He nodded at the older gentleman. "I thought I saw you going by the house this morning. Missus sent you out some lunch. She said you'd more than likely not have eaten."

"I forgot to get anything when I left the house." He took the large paper bag and put it on his lap. "You out looking at fences too? I've hit the ones behind me from your line on the property if you wanted to go this way. It's clean behind us."

Mason hoped that the man would say that he'd only brought him some food and go back, but he turned his horse in the same direction that his was going and said he'd ride along. Mason only nodded and gave his horse a little nudge to get him going. He reached into the bag and pulled out a large piece of angel food cake, and unwrapped it as he rode forward.

"My daughter comes home in a few weeks. She said she was coming to see us about something. I'm sure she's not happy about anything that might be happening between us and Dirk." Mason nodded as he took another bite of the soft moist cake. "She's a mite on the stubborn side. Not in the way that Dirk is, but a good deal more sassy. Dirk is just...he's got some strange ideas about what he wants and where he's headed."

"Dirk move out yet?" Landon said that he was still there. "I heard that he was having some problems finding him a place. I could help him find something if you want."

"Nah, he's going to do what he's going to do on his own. And we're not giving him any more money." Mason knew that was a sore point for the McBrides. "I have it and I want to keep it. Someday I might want to take the missus on a long vacation, and if Dirk had his way, he'd rather we spent it on him. Or take him along. I've done that kid wrong and now I'm paying for it."

"I don't know what you think you did, but you and Katie aren't to blame for what he is. Not by a long shot." Landon snorted and spit tobacco onto the ground before he looked at Mason. "Okay, I've heard things. And he never was one to be overly friendly when we were growing up. He has it in his head that his money—though I was never sure why it was his and not yours—but that his money was what made him special."

"He's a prick." Mason didn't say anything but stuffed the paper that the cake had been in back in the bag. Reaching for the sandwich that was there, also wrapped in waxed paper, he peeled it back to reveal a nice thick roast beef sandwich. "We should have made him finish college, or at least get a job. You'd think that he was too good to work the way he talks about it. Never even raised a finger to help out around the ranch. And to be truthful about it, I should have guessed he didn't want the ranch long before now."

Mason thought that if Dirk did take the ranch from his parents, it would be over almost as soon as he had to go out to the first chore. Dirk, as he'd always told them as kids, wasn't a rancher. He was more of the baron to one, and had shitheads to do the work for him. Good luck with that one, he'd thought even back then.

"You should just buy me out, Mason. I'd cut you a real good deal on the ranch and the steer." Mason stopped his horse and waited for Landon to stop and notice that he was no longer with him. "You want it, don't you? I mean, you do most of the work there anyway since I've got this cancer thing. I want to sell to you 'cause I know you will do right by it."

"I know nothing about steer, Landon. I can milk a cow and even farm a little, but nothing about raising steer to sell on the hoof." Landon laughed and Mason felt his face heat up. "Yeah, I'd love to buy you out, but I'd have no idea what to do with it."

"It's all cattle, Mason. And you sell the milk your cattle gives up now. Steer ain't no different. You're just selling the whole cow and not just a byproduct of it." Mason started to shake his head. "The barn is new with a heater in it. The house is up to date on all the appliances. We even put in new carpets last month with the idea of selling to somebody. You're the right person to buy it."

"How big?" He didn't have to explain to Landon what he wanted to know. The man could talk farm and ranches as well as he could. And when Landon looked out over the fence, the one that separated his ranch from the McBrides, he was almost afraid of the answer.

"Fifty acres of it belongs to my daughter. She wanted it and we gifted it to her some time ago. I'll talk to her about it when she comes in. Emma might not even want it anymore." Mason nodded, still waiting. "Dirk won't want any of it when it comes down to it. The money, sure, but not the land. He made that perfectly clear when I told him we might be selling. He don't know that it's you, of course, but he said that he...he told me he'd like his money in the form of cash. Little shit. I think he might think he's gonna get to stay on. I've yet to break that to him—"

"Landon, how big is the ranch? I've heard but I just don't...how big is it?" Mason had heard that it was the biggest ranch in the state. Other times he'd heard it was the biggest on this side of the United States. Either way, it was going to be a great many acres.

"Just over forty thousand acres." Mason heard the buzzing in his head and tried his best to ignore it so he could hear the man in front of him talking. "Covers three states, it does. Don't know why on earth we thought to have that much, but when we started out, we were young and thought more was better. Turned out that we didn't need nearly close to what we had, and started renting it out to other farmers and ranchers for the income. Not that we needed it, but the extra money was nice to have. Mason, you're turning green."

"Holy Christ, Landon. Three states? Mother fuck. I don't have that kind of money. Not even...I can't afford to buy you out." Landon nodded and turned his horse around to lead them. Mason caught up with him and felt badly that he couldn't help the man out. "I'm really sorry."

"It's not over. I'll think of something." Mason thought the man would have to think for a good long time for him to buy that much in the way of land. "The rent on the other parts would make a huge dent in the payments a month. Hell, one of them alone is damned near all of it. And they all have contracts should they decide they don't want to use it any more. I don't think that'll be a problem. You're a good man and most everyone knows that."

"The bank will require me to have a good deal more than I have right now." Which, Mason thought, was about a grand in his account. In the few weeks that he and Jace had been running the Rancher Association, he'd been paid well, but he had a lot of catching up to do. And buying a ranch, especially the size of the McBride ranch, wasn't even close to being on that list.

"Like I said, I'll have me a look into things. We'll figure something out." Landon stretched and looked over at him with a smile. "Maybe you could just take my daughter as your wife, and it'll all be yours free and clear. And we'd keep it all in the family. I wouldn't even care should you want to change it to the Double Deuce. Like that name just fine."

Mason laughed with him. There was no way he'd be marrying his daughter, and he was pretty sure Landon knew it. The man was making a joke, a poor one, as it felt for Mason, but a joke all the same. Mason had a mate out there somewhere, and Emma McBride wasn't it. He was sure of it. She was…well, she was a McBride, and he'd had his fill of the McBride children a long time ago in Dirk.

They rode along for another hour. It was getting close to dinner time, and Mason knew that he had to head home. He'd been hiding out long enough. But he also knew that should his family need him, someone would have gotten in touch with him and he'd have been right there. Mason needed this solitude, or what he'd had of it, more than he could have explained to his family.

Holly was going to have a baby in about eight months or so. She and Jace were so happy setting up their home and getting ready for it. The ranches, both of them, were doing better than they'd dreamed they would, and they'd even had to hire on some extra hands just to keep up.

Their dairy was going out all over the state now, and they'd been approached more than once by a few of the Mennonites around the area to sell them any extra they might have at the end of the day. So far it had been working out well for all of them. Very well.

"You and your family, you're doing well now. I gotta tell you, never thought of Jace as being a man like he is." Mason asked Landon what he meant. "Nothing bad. But to see him in a suit around town when he's at that big building…well, your momma, she'd be tickled pink, she would. Her boys working in a big corporations like that. And Jace and you seem to be doing a bang up job on the RA too. That Ranchers Association is helping a lot of people. And them dues we pay sure doesn't hurt nearly as bad as that banker was trying to do."

"Rogers." Landon nodded. "Yeah, he's not been heard from for a while now. People say he's taken off with their money. But that's dying down now too, since the bank is paying back what was ripped off from them."

Rogers was dead. Few people knew about it, but he was. Jace had worked with a couple of wolves he knew, and the man was fertilizer in some field somewhere with no part of him even big enough to search for. Some things like this were much better kept quiet. Landon might think it was a good thing, but Mason would never tell.

When they were near the ranch house, Landon shook his hand. "Thank you for the ride. Needed to get out more than I thought I did. Nice talking with a man who doesn't jabber all the time."

Mason thanked him and headed in the direction of his own ranch. Aunt Georgie was coming out on the porch when he got off his horse. She looked at him with her hand over her eyes to shield out the sun, and then smiled.

"I see you've been with Landon again. I swear to you that the man sits on his porch looking for one of you boys to ride by. He's a mite on the lonely side." Mason nodded as he tied his horse up. "You hungry? I can make you something before dinner."

"Nah. He brought me out a sandwich and some of Katie's cake." She asked him if it was her angel food. "Yeah. Man, that woman can bake like nobody's business."

"I hear that Emma can cook that well too. She don't much, I guess, but she can. Katie said she's coming home soon. Something about a sale." Mason only nodded. No sense in telling her of Landon's pipedream. "Did he ask you?"

Mason only nodded his head at her. Damn, but she could tell what was on a person's mind faster than they might know. Instead of answering her, he sat on the porch and let the swing rock him back and forth. When Aunt Georgie sat beside him, he just tilted his hat over his eyes for a moment.

"I can't swing it. As much as I'd like to, there is no way for me to do it." She only hummed her noncommittal answer. "Did you know that his land covers three states?"

"I did. I've lived here all my life too, you know." He eyed her under the brim of her hat. She was up to something, he just knew it. "That son of theirs, what do you know about him?"

"Dirk? Nothing much. He's a prick. We called him Dirk the Dick in school. I think he's closer to Jace's age. Told his daddy that he didn't want the ranch. I'm not sure, but I think Landon is sort of relieved that he doesn't." Aunt Georgie nodded. "I think he'd sell it off and walk away without a backward glance. Landon said that he wants money, not ground. Even told him when he sold out to give him cash for it. Like that man deserves even a dime off his dad's hard work."

"That's really too bad. There won't be any more dirt made in this world, but money will be the death of a lot of things." Mason said nothing. He'd heard her say that a great many times over the years. "If he can't find a buyer, do you know what he'll do with the land?"

"No. I didn't even ask him what he wanted for it. Forty thousand acres is more than I can handle even if he was selling it for a nickel an acre." She stopped swaying her feet and looked at him. "Yeah, that's what I said, forty thousand."

"Good heavens. I knew it was big, but...wow. You'd never know he had that much to look at him. I'd have thought...damn." Mason laughed when she cursed. It was something that she never did and rarely tolerated. "I'm guessing whoever gets it won't be ranching it. Probably turn it into a dude ranch or something."

When she left him there to tend to supper, he thought about the land. He was happy here. Not as happy as he'd be with all that extra land, but he could live without it. When Jace walked into the yard from his house, he wondered what the hell the man had been doing. He was covered from head to toe in mud.

"Can you help me out?" Mason stood and nodded. "There's a leak in the greenhouse and I need to get it fixed before Holly finds out I made it worse by not calling a plumber. I had no idea what the hell I was doing and should have...."

Mason walked back to Jace's house while he listened to him. This was what he needed. His family. And they were all nearby him too. When he got to the other ranch, he let his brother fiddle with the problem before he called in help. The plumber said he'd be there within the hour.

~~~

"Dirk, I don't have time for you right now." Not that she ever did, but right now Emma was too busy to even remember to eat the dinner she'd ordered. "Just get to the point so I can go home and put my feet up."

"He's kicking me out." Emma pulled the notepad to her and started making notes. Not on what her brother was saying, but on the case she'd had this afternoon. "Dad said he was selling out and that I'd have to find other digs."

"Dad's been saying he's selling out for years now." She nearly missed some of the wording on the computer when her brother started whining again. "Dirk, can this wait? I'm really swamped here, and I need to—"

"I think he's going to give it to the man next door. He's been sniffing around him for months now, and I think Dad is just going to give it to him." That got her attention. "His name is Douglas. They own the land that is close to ours. That guy has been up Dad's ass for a long time just waiting for him to turn the keys over to him. He'll take your land too, the part where you wanted to settle when you were ready. Like that's ever going to happen. You're a career woman."

Dirk had made career sound like it was some kind of disease or something. She loved working in the law firm, and hoped someday to hang out a sign that had her on name on it. But for now, she had some proving to do. Apparently even to her own brother.

"He can't sell my land. Dad gave me that." Dirk snorted. "He would have given you some too, Dirk, if he wasn't forever bailing your ass out of one thing or another. And me too. I'm not going to do this for you anymore. I've told you that."

"You'll help me. I'm Dirk McBride. And I don't know why he doesn't just give me what I want now. It's not like he needs all that money he has in the bank. Why do I have to wait until he's dead to get my half? He's being selfish." Emma could have told him he wasn't getting half, not even a third of the ranch or the money because of his antics, but she kept her mouth shut as he continued talking. Finally she cut him off.

"I'm coming home in a few weeks. Sooner if I can get this case finished. I'll look into it. I swear." He said something about taking care of it himself, but she told him to stay out of it. "Dad isn't going to sell the ranch today or tomorrow. Just give me some time to look into this, and for Christ's sake, stay out of it. Dad said if you did one more thing to piss him off, he'd cut you out without a dime. And you'd be living on the streets. I'd believe him if I was you, Dirk. He's pretty pissed off at you."

"So? Like I care what he thinks about doing to me. I'm his only son. He'll have to take me back into our house. Even if he doesn't, you will." Emma didn't tell him she could and would leave him to his own devices in a heartbeat if he fucked with her. "Mom and Dad are not young anymore and if they die, I'll be all right and as rich as I'd ever want to be. I just want him to acknowledge that I'm a grown man and should have my money now. I've got things I want to do with it now, not later. Being a McBride comes with a certain price, and Dad is cramping it all up for me."

Dad was cramping it up? Just last week she'd had to go to court with Dirk to get him out of much more trouble than a man his age should be in. At thirty-five, Dirk acted more like a ten-year-old than his age, and his run-ins with the law were starting to get harder and harder to get him out of. But no more. She'd told him that when they'd left the courthouse then.

"I'm not doing this again. You will have to find someone else to represent you. I'm not doing it." He'd only told her to be serious. "I am being serious, Dirk. I'm finished bailing you out as much as Dad and Mom are. You fuck up again and I want you to forget my number."

Even when he left her to go and celebrate, she knew that in short order he was going to be in more trouble. But she'd already talked to her parents and they had agreed

15

with her. It was time to cut the ties and make him suffer for what he'd been doing.

By the time she was caught up for the day, it was nearly ten o'clock. Christ, if this didn't help her make partner, she had no idea what would. Emma was going to her car when she heard someone coming down the lane she was in. Instead of getting in, being trapped in her car, she pulled out her gun and turned to look at the person as she put her hand down beside her coat.

"Hello." She didn't say anything to the man but nodded. "I'm new here. And I think I forgot where I parked my car."

"I can't help you." He nodded and took a step toward her. Emma brought the gun up. "I'm registered to use and carry this. You come one step closer and I will put a bullet between your eyes."

Lifting her camera up, she started pushing the button on it to take pictures. She knew that there was a camera right behind her, but she didn't want to take any chances that it missed his face. The man backed up but didn't leave.

"You're not at all friendly, are you?" Emma listened hard to his voice, the way he spoke and any movements that might give the police some information later. Emma only hoped she'd be around to tell them. "I'm here to talk to you, nothing more. Put the camera down and we'll go somewhere and talk."

"Yeah, that's so not going to happen." He looked to his left and she didn't. It was something that she had read in a transcript once as how they'd gotten the victim by misdirection. When he looked back at her, she had an eerie feeling that she was in more trouble than she'd first thought. The footsteps coming toward them had her shifting on her feet.

"Miss, are you all right?" She didn't know this man either. "Want me to call the police? Is this man bothering you?"

Emma didn't take her eyes off either man but did glance at her phone once. She was pressing the button to call the police herself when the first man leapt at her. She fired her gun just as the phone call was answered.

"Parker Building garage. Shots fired. Man down." She felt her head explode in pain when she hit something hard behind her. "Emma McBride, two men are attacking me on the fifth level b-side."

Emma fired her gun twice more. She knew that she'd hit one of the men but was not sure which. Someone started to drag her across the floor and she kicked out, hitting something hard enough to have the person let her go. Backing up again, she tried to see where they were, but her vision was blurred and her head was making her sick. Holding out her gun, she fired again and thought that someone had hit the ground from the sound of it. Then the sound of sirens started and she heard more running feet. Emma crawled backwards to the wall and cradled her gun and phone in her hands.

It was perhaps ten minutes before she heard a car come to a screeching halt close by. Emma was beginning to feel sick now, her body hurt, and she thought for sure her arm was broken, if not badly sprained. When someone said her name, she didn't move, didn't speak, but waited.

"Miss McBride, it's Officer James O'Donnell. I'm with the police department. Tell me where you are and I'll come to you." She didn't move yet. This could be another ploy. But he was suddenly standing in front of her, his shadows moving in a way that made her sick. Emma lifted her gun.

"I'm not going to hurt you. I'm going to hand you my badge. You can't see, can you?"

"I hurt." He said he could tell that. "I don't know if I should trust you. Those men, they were going to...I don't know what, but I shot at them."

"You did at that." His radio started talking, and she heard him talking to it. "Found Miss McBride; two down, one dead and it doesn't look good for the other guy either. We'll need an ambulance and a coroner."

"I'm not dead." He laughed and told her that it wasn't for her. "I don't know what they wanted with me. I don't...I was working late."

"I'm going to ask you to put down your gun, miss. The medics won't help you unless you do. And I can't let them." Emma curled the gun closer to her chest. "I'm sorry, Miss McBride, but you're going to have to let it go."

"Don't hurt me, please?" He assured her that he wouldn't. Giving him her weapon was the hardest thing she'd ever done, and as soon as it was out of her hand, everything faded out. *Christ, I really am hurt*, she thought.

CHAPTER 2

Dirk came out of his room and looked around the house. There wasn't anyone around and he was sort of pissed about that. Usually his mom or dad was right there when he came out of his room, ready to blast him about the lateness of the hour or something that they had to pay for. This time he had a line all ready for them. Going to the kitchen, he found not only the cook but the woman who cleaned his room. *What the fuck is going on*, he thought, but didn't ask. Not the help. They were too beneath him to be even considered human. They looked like they had been to a funeral, however, and he wondered if his dad had finally died and left him all the money. Dirk moved out of the kitchen and to the dining room. He was hungry and wanted to be served right now.

He was brought his coffee first. When the maid or whatever the hell she was left him, he sipped it and tried to think of something to bitch about when he was brought his food. That was when he saw the note addressed to him propped up against the salt shaker. Dirk ignored it until he had his cereal, and even then he simply moved it out of his way and put milk in his bowl before he decided it was time. Opening it, he pulled out the short note in his dad's handwriting and decided that whatever it said couldn't be as important as his dad had thought it should be to him.

Emma is in the hospital. Someone tried to hurt her last night, and your mother and I have gone to see her.

Figures, thought Dirk. *Anything to get out of helping me out.* His sister was a real bitch. He read the rest of his dad's note to him.

We should be back in a few days to a week. I'll let you know if it's longer. Mason Douglas will be coming by to look in on things. *Do not* give him a hard time. He's doing us a favor.

His dad had underlined *do not* like he was serious. Dirk was too. When they started taking him seriously, he would them. Looking up when someone entered the room, he nearly ignored the butler, but he cleared his throat.

"Sir, your father is on the phone. He would like to speak to you." Dirk looked down at his cereal bowl, empty except for some left over milk. If he talked to his dad, it would no doubt be removed when he returned, as if he'd never been in this room. Dirk wanted to be thought of as important all the time. It was his right as a McBride. He started to tell the man to tell Dad he'd call him back, but the man spoke first. "He said it's important."

"Damn it all to hell." He got up and made sure that he knocked his bowl over. It would be a mess when he returned, so why not have someone clean it up for him? Going to the phone in the hall, he picked it up just in time to hear his dad talking to someone about transfers. "Dad. I don't have time to run to the phone when you want something. Just have one of the servants do whatever it is you want. That's what you pay them for, isn't it? Besides, I just got up and was eating."

"Did you get my note? And it's nearly two in the afternoon, Dirk. You should have been up hours ago. Damn it, son, what the hell am I going to do with you?" Dirk started to tell him to leave him the fuck alone, but Dad spoke first. "Emma has been hurt, like I told you. But they're going to let us bring her home tomorrow. Has Mason...? Never mind. He gets up at the crack of dawn like most ranchers, and would have been there and gone by now."

"Dad, I'm working on things too." When asked, Dirk had nothing to tell his dad, but he changed the subject. "You said that Emma was hurt. What did she do now? Fall again? She's the stupidest woman I know."

The line was suddenly humming, and he realized that they'd been disconnected. Putting the phone back in the cradle, he went back to the dining room, pleased that not only had the mess been cleaned up, but the table cloth was changed as well...actually, not so much changed as gone.

When his coffee and donuts were brought to him this time, he ate them quickly. If his dad was right and it was after noon, then he had to get to town. Dirk had a meeting with a couple of people and he didn't want to be late.

Going out to the garage made him go back into the house and look for that damned butler.

"Where's my car?" No one said a word. "You do know what a car is, right? Four tires and metal around it. Bright red with...where is my fucking car?"

"I'm sorry, sir, but a taxi conveyed you home last night...this morning. I had to pay him for you when you didn't yourself." There was a tone there, but Dirk was going to ignore it for now. "He must have brought you a great distance, as it cost well over two hundred dollars."

Dirk couldn't remember coming home, much less taking a taxi. And where the hell had he left his car? He had no way of going into town now, as his dad had also removed all the keys to the other cars in the garage. He knew where to find them, but the lock was one that he'd not been able to break into. So he was stuck.

If he called a cab to come and get him, he'd have to pay. Borrowing money from the help wasn't going to happen. None of them would help him out since his dad had told them not to. And since his dumbass sister was hurt, neither Dad nor Mom would give him any either. Fucking bullshit was what this was. His dad was just going to have to give him more money to carry around. This was just stupid to have him ask every time he needed more, and lately that was getting to be hard too. His father had to know that being a McBride like him, he had to have money all the time.

He was nearly to his room again when someone knocked on the front door. The butler went to answer it, and Dirk stayed on the stairs. Since his family was gone, that made him in charge. Even when they were home, Dirk knew that he was the one that would inherit all this, so he was, in his mind, in charge. Going down the stairs when a man was let in, Dirk nearly went back up when he saw who it was.

"Mason? What the hell are you doing here?" Mason didn't answer him but did cock that fucking brow at him. He'd done that in school too when he felt that Dirk was beneath him, which wasn't possible since Dirk had all the money and the last name of McBride. "Dad said you were going to work around here while he was gone. There's no reason for you to be coming in the house or in the front door. The help uses the back door."

The butler inhaled sharply, but Mason only stood there and smiled at him. Dirk had hated that entire Douglas family his whole life. They had nothing, came from nothing, and he felt like they were nothing. But they were never without girls, always had what he wanted, and the fuckers seemed to always be looking down their noses at him. Him, Dirk Dwight McBride.

"I've come to see Mr. Fox." Dirk asked him who the hell that was before he could think about it. "It's this man right here. Don't you even know the name of the people who work for you?"

"Like I care." Dirk came down the stairs, but not all the way. Had he stood on the same level as Mason the man would have towered over him, and Dirk hated that. "What the hell do you need to see the help about? You looking for pointers on how to be a good servant, Mason?"

"I'm here to see him, not you." Mason started for the kitchen, no doubt going to have a free meal on them, and Dirk followed. He kept his distance, but he did go in. By the time he got there, Mason had removed his hat and was under the sink. He was talking to Fox, no doubt, about what he was seeing. "Yeah, it'll need to be replaced. You can call out a plumber, but I can have one of my brothers come over in a bit and fix this. Won't take much. A washer or two and it'll be good as new."

When Mason stood up, Dirk backed up. He hated to be intimated like this, and Mason did it every time he saw him. The fact that he had a good five or so inches on him notwithstanding, the man outweighed him by at least sixty pounds of muscle. The fucker was just a lowlife, and that was another thing to add to his list of things to hate them for. The Douglases were beneath him, especially Mason, and it was time they figured that out.

"You're to come into the house from the rear from now on, Mason. I don't want your kind coming in the front of the house and scaring away decent people." Mason just laughed at him. "You think that I'm not being serious? Try me. I'm the head of his house when my father is gone, and it's about time you started to realize your place. And as soon as he gives me the money I have coming to me, I'm going to make you sorry."

"My place?" Dirk nodded and nearly whimpered when the entire staff left the two of them standing there. "My place is where I want it to be, you little piece of shit. And the next time you address me this way, you'd better be ready to back up your words. I'm not some little piss ant that you can order around because you have a little bit of money. I'm not one you want to fuck with. You hear me?"

"I'll tell my dad."

As soon as he said it, Dirk realized what a mistake he'd made. It was childish and stupid. He was an adult and he was fucking sick of people treating him like he was nothing. When he doubled up his fist to hit Mason, Dirk would have sworn that Mason tilted his chin in a way that sort of offered it up. But when his hand connected with the bigger man's face, Dirk knew the real meaning of pain. There was no time to wallow in his hurt…the next thing he knew he was on the floor with Mason on him. His knee in his back was making it so that not only couldn't Dirk move, but it was difficult to breathe as well. The sound of a door opening somewhere nearby had him crying out for them to fucking help him. But Mason spoke.

"He hit me." Someone asked if he was all right, and Dirk thought it was Fox. "Yeah, just a little bump on the chin. I think he might be hurting more than me. I don't know what the fuck he was thinking hitting someone with my size on him is beyond me." Fox just laughed when Mason did.

"Let me up and I'll show you how hurt I am." That laugh again, and Dirk decided that he was going to fucking kill them all. "Fox, you're fired. And Mason, I'll see you in jail for this. You motherfucker, get the hell off me. I'm Dirk McBride, and you will not treat me this way."

He was let go, but Dirk couldn't move. He hurt. Everywhere. And when he rolled over, he found himself in the room alone. Rolling to his belly again, he had to use the chair, then the table, to get to his feet, and even then he staggered just a little.

Making his way to his room, he was glad that he didn't encounter anyone on the way. Pissed beyond anything he'd ever been before, he headed to the shower to try and work some of the soreness out of his body. His hand was broken, he just knew it. When he was cleaned up and dressed, he made his way to the kitchen again. Someone was going to take him to the hospital or he'd call an ambulance. Either way, Mason was going to get the bill. There was no way his money was going for this.

Fox took him to the hospital, but he never spoke to him. Not a single word passed his lips even when Dirk asked him direct questions. This shit was going to stop too, and as soon as his dad got back, he was going to demand again that he be given money so he could hire his own staff. As he was being dropped off in front of the emergency room, he turned back to the man and sneered at him.

"I'm going to find my own way back home. Don't wait up. And if I have to take a cab back because you did something with my car, I'm going to expect you to pay for that as well." Fox never looked at him or acknowledged him at all. When Dirk asked if he'd heard him, the man actually flipped him off and took off driving with him still holding on to the door. Dirk might have fallen had he not been quick on his feet.

Dirk was at the desk waiting for one of the bitches behind the counter to help him when he realized two things; he had no phone and he had no wallet. He was fucked no matter how he looked at it. There was no way he could call for his sister...no, that wasn't going to work either. She'd been hurt, or so he'd been told. These people were going to have to learn that as Dirk McBride, he knew things they'd never understand.

"May I help you?" The woman that stood in front of him looked like she could have beaten a bear with a switch and come out the winner. "You got a tongue in that head of yours, boy? Or you just looking at the view?"

"I think my hand is broken, and you have no right to talk to me that way. I'm Dirk McBride of the McBride billions." She only huffed at him and told him to fill out the paperwork on the clipboard. "I just told you that I think my fucking hand is—"

"You want me to come over this counter at you and show you what a broken face feels like, boy?" Dirk shook his head as he took a step back. "Get that butt of yours over there in a chair and fill this out. Then when your number is called, we'll have a look at it. But you give me any more trouble and I will hurt you worse than you are right now."

Dirk went to one of the little plastic chairs and sat down. He tried twice to pick up the fucking pen and couldn't do it. He supposed he really wasn't trying all that hard, but his temper was getting the better of him. This was no way to treat a McBride, damn it. People were going to start paying attention to him, or else. Dirk left the clipboard there with the pen and left. He'd find someone to help him and then show them all.

~~~

Emma was more embarrassed than she was hurting. She did hurt, but the fact that her parents had to be called in made her feel ridiculous. She took great pride in taking care of herself. Emma looked at her mom when she said her name.

"The doctor is talking to you." Flushing again, Emma looked at the woman who'd been really nice to her since she'd woken up. "Honey, are you sure you want to go home so soon?" Emma nodded before looking at the doctor.

"I'm sorry." Doctor Silva nodded at her as if she might understand where her mind had been. "I've been really busy at work lately, and I think I might have to leave before dark from now on. It was really late."

"Yes, so the police said. But they have cleared you of all that happened, so you're free to go as far as I'm concerned. I would like for you to rest a few days before taking on any other would-be rapists, if you don't mind." Emma nodded and shivered. "You did a good thing, Emma. Had you not killed them, they would have surely killed you."

That didn't make the fact that she'd killed two men any better. The police had been in earlier and asked her several questions. They have given her phone back to her, minus the pictures she'd taken, of course, and had told her that the video from the garage had confirmed her story. She was so glad, but now she had to live with what she'd done.

Taking the bag from her mom when the doctor left, she headed to the bathroom. Getting dressed was harder than she'd thought it would be. Even with the soft terrycloth pants and shirt her mom had bought for her, she was still struggling with them. And she was so tired too. Every little thing seemed to drain her. When she was finally dressed, she came out of the bathroom and sat in the room's only chair, and contemplated how to not wear shoes home.

Taking her shoes from her lap, her mom sat down on the floor to help her. "I was terrified when we got that call. I know you're a big girl and all, but you're still my little girl and I worry about you. And your father nearly had a stroke when I woke him up to come here. You'd have thought that someone had kidnapped you the way he was going on. I had to have the limo bring us. He wasn't fit to drive."

"I'm okay, Mom. I took those defense classes and I have…had a gun." The police would return that later, they told her. And one of them even commented on what a great shot she'd been. "I'm fine other than a sprained wrist and a concussion, and a few bumps and bruises that will heal soon. I'll be as good as new."

"Your office manager is here." Her dad came into the room like he did everything, powerfully and full of energy. "Can I let them in?"

Nodding, she started to stand up, but her mom pushed her back into the chair. When Mr. Foster, the president of their firm, came in, she tried to stand again and he told her to stay where she was. He was with his secretary, a woman that Emma had never liked.

"I just had a long conversation with my security firm. They are going to…well, let's just say that you're never going to run into this sort of issue again." She nodded and started to tell him what she'd told the cops…she shouldn't have been working so late. "You will also be escorted out to your car from now on; everyone will if they work past six o'clock. Which brings up my second reason for being here. I had no idea you were working so many hours."

"I love my job." He laughed and sat on the edge of the bed. "I really do. I love working for this firm and what I do there. It's my fault and no one else's that I was there so late."

"No, it wasn't your fault, and I'm looking into that as well. How long have you been carrying Mr. Patterson?" She didn't answer, but he must have seen something in her face. "I see. That long, huh? I've had my suspicions, but until now, until I had someone go to your office and…how can you work in there? And I'm working on some other issues that have come up regarding him as well."

"It's what I was given when I started there. It suits my needs and it's really close to the vending machine when I forget to eat something. I try not to, but I get caught up in my work." He nodded but said nothing more. "Mr. Patterson has been giving me some advice on things that I've taken to heart."

"I just bet he has. You might change your tune when you hear that he said that he's been having to redo your work since you've been there, and that he has had it on his list of things to do to fire you for months now." She glared at no one in particular, and Mr. Foster laughed again. "I can see that you're not at all happy with his assessment of you and your work ethics. No matter, in a few weeks—less if I can help it along—Peter will have shown his true colors…if he hasn't already. The man is a lazy lawyer and has been riding on my firm's good name for too long now."

"I don't know what to say to that." Mr. Foster said that she had no reason to speak about him. "I'm coming back to work as soon as my doctor releases me. I'll work more to make up for the time I've missed. I know that I have some vacation time coming, but I won't be gone that long."

"Another reason I'm here. I've come to some decisions while I've been hearing about you. You're up for partner in a few months, and I'd like to offer that to you now." Her dad whooped and she turned and smiled at him when he apologized. "You've raised a very intelligent and well thought of young daughter; you should be proud. I'm proud of her myself."

"Damned right we did. Her mother and I worked hard on...nah, it's all my girl there." Her dad kissed her on the forehead and reached for her mom's hand. "She's the best thing that we've ever done, this one is. And you'd not do no better than having her as a partner."

Emma flushed when her dad gushed over her. She wasn't used to high praise. It felt good to be acknowledged about her job, but being offered the job she wanted was more than she could have hoped for.

"I don't know what to say. Thank you. But if this is because I was hurt, I'd rather get it on my merit, not this." She started to stand again and had to sit down quickly. Mr. Foster stood and helped her back to her bed, and then stood over her. "I'm going to be fine."

"I know that you are. And as your boss, I'm going to give you an order that will keep you healthy too...starting the moment you get to your parents' house. I'm assuming that's where you're headed?" She shook her head and her mom and dad nodded. "All right then, when you get to your parents' house, where you will be going, you'll rest. And watch stupid programs on the television. You're going to eat when you want and as much as you want. And you'll do it for a month. And so you know, you being hurt only expedited this promotion. You're doing an excellent job, and I've had the pleasure of seeing you in action a couple of times in court. You know what you're doing, and you have no problem with getting your hands dirty. The kind of person I want working with me, not for me. I need you on my team, Emma, and I'll be happy if you say yes. But you're still taking a month off."

"A month? I can't be there for a month. A week tops, but not a month. I'll be so behind that—" Mr. Foster cut her off with a lift of his hand. "Sir, that's a long time to be away."

"It would have been a good deal longer had you been killed last night." Emma shivered at the image of the two men coming at her. "Now, as I was saying, a month off with pay. And while you're gone, there will be some changes made to where you're working, how long you're working, and if you trust me, I'll hire you someone to keep your desk cleared of most of the debris on it. You do like your tea, don't you?"

"I do." Mr. Foster stood up, and she watched him shake hands with her dad. She was overwhelmed right now, and she wasn't sure what to think. But the thing that was forefront in her mind was, she was a partner. A flipping partner. When he was gone, her dad laughed like a loon and her mom told her how proud she was.

"My little girl a partner in a big law firm. Just look at that. And it only took you…what? Four years?" She told her dad that it took ten. "Four, ten. I don't care, you did it. I'm so proud of you, honey, I could just bust."

The ride home was made better by a quick stop at the drug store. Her pain pills kicked in about the time the big, comfortable car was getting on the highway. Closing her eyes, she only opened them once when she heard her dad cursing, but only smiled and let the drugs take her away. By the time she was being carried to her bedroom, by a handsome cowboy no less, she had decided that she really liked being doped up a little and fell right to sleep again when he put her in the bed.

The dream started out like it always did. She was trapped. Breathing was hard, and she couldn't see anything. Her fingers were raw from trying to climb out of the long dark hole she was in, and she cried out when something touched her legs. There was no way for her to see what it was, and she knew that she more than likely didn't want to know. As a scream started to build in her lungs, she could feel the terror in her heart, making it pound too hard and too fast. When she let it go, the scream waking her from the nightmare, she sat in the middle of the bed. Her bed. Her room. When the door to her room slammed back against the wall, her father stood there with his gun in his hand, wearing his boxers and tee-shirt.

"Where is he?" Emma asked him who. "Whoever had you screaming the house down. Christ girl, you nearly gave us a heart attack. There ain't nobody in here?"

"No. It's a dream, just a bad dream." He turned on the light and shooed her mom back to bed. "I'm sorry I woke you. I haven't…it's been a while since I've had bad dreams."

"You still think about the time that Dirk shoved you down that hole, don't you?" Emma nodded. "That boy is not right, honey. To have done that to his little sister and you being so young. You were smart to keep screaming for us. It was the only way we found you. But I got you here now, and I just might keep you."

When he put the gun by the door and came into her room, she snuggled down under the covers and watched him sit in the chair by the bed. She watched him just sitting there watching her, his blinks getting longer and longer until he yawned. When she did as well, Emma felt safe and rolled to her side and let sleep take her. She knew that if she had any more dreams tonight, her daddy was there to keep her safe.

CHAPTER 3

"I'm going to go over and see the McBride's daughter, Emma. You want to come with me?" Holly thought that Georgie knew the McBride's, but after talking to her this morning, she realized that while she knew of them, the boys had known only the son and dad. "You should come with me. We can go to lunch if you want. My treat."

"You always treat even when I ask you to go." Georgie was snapping green beans for dinner, and Holly wondered what Jace was making them. He loved to cook, and on Thursdays the cook was off so he did it for them. It was always some recipe that he found or someone had given him. And it was always delicious.

"You know you want to." Georgie shook her head. "Come on. I want to go, and you're making it hard on me to go shopping beforehand. I need to get a few things at the store, and there's that nice little shop that opened that I want to go to. It's called Indigo Dreams."

"Really, honey, I don't want to go. Your dad is coming over tonight and I wanted to make his favorite dinner. He's been keeping me company while the boys are out." Mason and the rest of the men were out gathering some strays for the Mitchell farm. Mr. Mitchell had fallen ill a week ago, and he couldn't get out just yet. Holly wondered if he was going to be able to get back into ranching again. She'd never cared for him. She had no idea why, but he'd always made her feel dirty. Not that she wanted him to be sick or anything.

Holly drove herself to town. She was still scared at times. Jeff would be in the face of one of the strangers on the street, or his mom would seem to leap out at her in the strangest places. Neither of them were there, of course. Margaret Hardgrave was dead, and Jeff was still in a mental hospital. He'd had a break down when they started finding the bodies at his mom's place. Four bodies, one of them his father's, and he'd just gone over the edge. But there was hope. The doctor had told them that he'd recover. Not soon, but he'd be able to function outside the nursing home he was in, a nursing home specially set up for people that had lost their way.

Stopping at the little shop first to get a gift for her friend, she found so many things that she had a pile of them when she realized she was having fun. Things had been a little tense around the ranch lately. Not with her and Jace, but with the business of dealing with the bank and the mill.

The new banker had been working hard to gain the confidence of the town's people. She and Jace had hosted a big party to get the town to come by and meet him, and that had gone a long way. But the mill was still closed, and with it all the needs of the town. It was costly for them to have to go all the way across the state to get supplies, and Jace and his brother Gerard had set up a storefront in an empty warehouse that was doing a booming business. Holly thought that Gerard was having fun at it too, being a shopkeeper.

Going to the counter, she waited as the person in front of her was checked out, and smiled when a woman came from the back room and started bagging things up for the customer. She knew she was the owner of the place right away.

"You've done well in picking things out for this place." The woman flushed. "I'm Holly Douglas; my family has the ranch just outside of town."

"Doris Roman, and this is my daughter Tessa. We're having...I hope you buy like this all the time." Trouble. Holly knew the sound of someone discouraged about their business. It had been a way of life around here for far too long. "That sounded just rude, didn't it? I'm sorry."

"No worries. I was thinking of how nice your shop is and how much fun I'm having. If you don't mind me asking, are you new to town?" She told her that they'd moved in about a month ago. They were using the upstairs as their home for now. "You're doing well then?"

Doris just looked dejected before she spoke. "Not so much. I mean, I know that it's only been a couple of weeks and we get a lot of traffic, but not many of them are buying. I was hoping we could do this instead of working in a factory or something. Tessa here is working now for the lady at the diner to help out. And I'm making stuff to sell that's not moving."

"You make all this?" Doris told her that she made about seventy-five percent, the rest she had to buy. "It's beautiful. I think I might be in here a lot."

Doris showed her around the shop and pointed out the things that she'd made, and a few that she'd repurposed from auctions or such. An old trunk was filled with finger towels that had been decorated with hand stitching. A lamp with a handmade lampshade was covered in buttons of all kinds. Doris was talented, that was for sure, and she had a good eye for art.

"Have you a webpage?" Holly had only asked her casually and turned when the woman didn't answer her. "Doris?"

"I can't read." Her face deepened to a dark red as the woman realized what she'd just confessed. "I didn't get much in the way of education when the babies came along. By then it was too late. My husband was gone and I had me five children to care for. He took it all from us that might have helped us out. But we made it, and I'm very proud of my kids."

"As well you should be. Not many could start a new business like you have and try to make a success of it. Good for you." Doris told her she was proud of them and that the boys, all four of them, had moved to other states when they got good jobs. "I'm assuming that Tessa is your youngest? And I can tell that if your sons are anything like their mother, they're doing well now too."

"They're good boys, all of them. They send me money when they can, but three of them have families of their own, and I won't take what they can use. The other one, my youngest boy, he's in college. He's doing really well and someday he's going to be a fine doctor. I don't want you to think I'm asking you to feel sorry for me. I've done right by them."

"Well, of course you have. And I'd punch anyone who said anything different." Doris nodded and left her there when her daughter said she needed help with the phone. Holly contacted Jace and told him what she wanted to do.

I'm all for it. But will you let me have her investigated first? She told him she was going to do it regardless. *I already figured that out, honey. I just want to make sure, okay?*

You should see the things she's made. I'm telling you, Jace, if she had an online store, she'd be rich in a month. And this place would just be a place for the leftovers if she had any. He told her to go for it. *Thank you. I knew you'd see it my way.*

Now if you can get someone to open a play shop, I'll be a happy man. Her body warmed at the thought of going to a place where they could play. *Holly, I can feel how aroused you are. If you keep that up, I'm going to leave the men here and come find you.*

No, but as soon as you come home tonight, I'm going to be in the woods behind the house waiting for you. His low growl had her wet in seconds. Telling him to behave didn't help either. When Doris returned, Holly had to think how to speak, then what to say to her. Jace's laughter didn't help at all.

"I'm going to help you." Doris was shaking her head, and Holly nodded. "I am. Now, sometime today if he can swing it, a man by the name of…no, that won't work. He's with Dad on that trip. Let me see…okay. Irwin Henderson is going to contact you. He'll come with someone, but I'm not sure who yet, but—"

"Slow down. Who are you sending and why? I'm telling you right now, I don't have any money to spare, and what I do have is going to books for my daughter. Whatever you're selling, Mrs. Douglas, I just can't do." Holly laughed and told her that it was going to be great working with her. "Working with me? I don't understand. I don't…what's going on?"

By the time she'd gotten in touch with Irwin, she was nearly finished explaining what she had in mind. Doris was still leery about it, but Tessa was asking questions like a pro. When Irwin showed up an hour later with a camera man and a laptop, Tessa was lining things up she thought should be put on the webpage first. Holly left them to it, feeling the best she'd felt in a long time.

Going down the long drive to the McBride ranch made her think of her own home…not the one that she'd grown up in, but the one that she and Jace had now. It was spectacular, and she loved every inch of it. And the greenhouse that Jace had had put in for her was her sanctuary. Soon they'd be adding to the house with the baby. That had her both nervous and excited.

Parking the car, she went up to the door and was let in by Mr. Fox. She laughed when she realized that he wasn't just Mr. Fox, but he was one. He grinned at her as well.

"I'd heard that you'd made some changes in your life. I'm happy to see that they're suiting you well." Holly told him that she was having a good time. "Very good, miss. I'm very happy for you."

"I came to see Emma. She and I have known each other just about forever, I think. How's she doing?" He told her she was resting but wanting to get out. "I bet. She never was one to sit still for long."

Holly was taken to the living room and brought some tea and scones. Mrs. Baker had always been the best cook, and she wondered if she'd tell the recipe to Jace so that he could make these too. When Emma came in, Holly nearly swallowed her food whole.

"Yeah, I know, I look like shit." Emma hobbled into the room and, after sharing a hug with Holly, sat on the couch near the fireplace. "I've been thinking that the doctor might have been right in telling me that the worst was yet to come. Christ, I hurt in places that I had no idea that they had names for."

"You look good other than you're beat to shit." They both laughed. "How are you, really? I'd heard that you were mugged, but this looks like more."

"I don't know what they intended other than they were going to get me. The police said that they thought rape and murder; nice combo, right? But I don't think they expected me to fight back or have a gun."

Holly had heard that as well. That Emma had killed both men who had attacked her. And when Logan had gotten home yesterday after helping the McBride's put Emma to bed, he said that she looked like someone had run over her. Logan had wanted to go and find the men and kill them again, he'd been so upset.

They talked for a time, and Holly gave Emma her gift...well, gifts. She'd gotten her the lovely lap blanket with the hand embroidered work done on it, and a basket of homemade soaps. Emma said she was looking forward to using them.

They talked for an hour, catching up on things. Holly wasn't surprised to hear that she'd been offered the partnership in the firm she worked for, and Emma was thrilled for her and Jace about the new baby. It wasn't until someone started shouting from the hall that she realized that Mr. McBride was home, as well as Dirk.

Holly had never cared for Dirk. Few people did, she supposed. He was an ass and a jerk. Dirk also treated everyone like they weren't good enough to be around him, including his parents. Holly had always thought that someone should take him down a few notches, but so far as she knew, it had never happened. When Emma said her name, she looked back at her.

"He's gotten himself in trouble again. And I'm not going to go to court with him. Not that I could, but he's pissed." Holly nodded. "He's no different now than when he was little, in case you didn't notice."

"What did he do now?" Emma told her that he'd been caught stealing a car. "I thought he had one. I've seen him around town driving it. Did he wreck it?"

"No. He lost it. And I don't mean that he lost it as in he doesn't know where he parked it. Though from what I understand from Fox, he did do that. But he lost it playing poker. Dad won't buy him a new one and he thinks that he should, of course. Then there's the money he owes for breaking up a bar that night too. I can't understand how he's part of my parents DNA." Holly didn't either. "And now Dad is kicking his ass out. As of this morning, the locks have been changed and all the accounts have been barred from him. He's flat broke and out on the streets."

"Your mom must be heart broken." Emma told her that she was glad for it really. "I see. Well, then good. And so you know, Mason, my brother-in-law, had a run in with him the other day. I guess he hit him and then fired Fox."

"I bet that was great. Dirk is a bully and he's always been one. I was going to court for him weekly for a while there, and then I told him I was done bailing his ass out. You can imagine how well that went over."

Before she could say anything to Emma, the door to the room was shoved open and there stood Dirk. He'd not aged well since she'd seen him last. Dirk wasn't fat, but he had a gut that she thought of as a beer gut. But his clothing was pressed, his shirt was done up nicely, and his shoes had a shine on them that was nearly blinding. That was another thing about Dirk. He spent more money on his appearance than he did anything else. Well, not his money, but Mr. McBride's. She remembered a time when she'd been shopping for a gift for her dad when he'd come into the same store.

He'd gone from stack to stack, picking up shirts and tossing them back unfolded and a mess. Ties were stripped from their hangers and then dropped on the floor. When a clerk asked him if she could help, Dirk had turned to her and said he was Dirk McBride, and that he knew more about clothing than the clerk did. Dirk had ended up spending just over five grand in the store, then gave the clerk a hard time because she wouldn't give him an advance on his credit card. When he sat down beside Holly, she moved away.

"Hello beautiful. Where have you been all my life?" Holly looked at Emma, then back at Dirk. "I'm homeless now...well, for a little while anyway. My dad seems to think that having me under the roof is going to take all his money. Like that's going to happen. And besides, I'm his son. I deserve to live where I want. How about I come and stay with you until my dad gets a clue?"

"No, Dirk, you cannot." He frowned at her, obviously not used to people telling him no. "And you should have a good deal more respect for your parents. They're good people and have worked hard to make their money." Holly stood up and went to sit on the couch with Emma. It was more to protect her than to get away from Dirk. But when he sneered at her, she thought he was just like a spoiled child.

"Respect for my parents? When they give me what's mine and are both dead and cold in their graves, then perhaps I'll think kindly of them. But they're kicking me out and making all these...demands. Why should I get a job? I'm Dirk McBride. And a house? Please. I live here, it's my style. They're going to regret this."

When he just sat there staring at them, Holly looked at Emma. She was crying, and Holly held her. To have an asshole like him for a brother would make her cry too. Then she'd kick his ass for being that way. Holly decided to let Jace know what was going on here, and soon.

~~~

Dirk stared at the lovely woman who had moved away from him. He thought she looked familiar, but had no idea right now from where. Her being married didn't stop him from flirting with her, but when he tried to touch her by moving across the room to talk to Emma, she growled at him.

"Who the fuck do you think you are?" He stood up, and she did too. "What the fuck are you even doing in my house? Get your ass out of—"

"Dirk, shut up."

He looked at his sister when she spoke. She'd been getting really mouthy with him too, lately, and he was sick of it. First there was his dad and whatever he was going to do about getting him out of his house, and now this shit. The entire family had gone over the deep end if they thought they could order Dirk McBride around and get away with it. Moving to the couch where his sister was still seated, Dirk drew back his hand to hit Emma when he was suddenly on the floor.

"You touch any of these people and I will tear your throat out." Dirk lay very still...not because he was afraid of her—no, never that—but because he wanted his family to see how guests were treating him. But his sister said nothing as the woman continued. "You think I'm kidding you, Dirk the Dick?"

That name. That fucking horrible name he'd been called since he'd been a kid. Dirk roared out his anger but couldn't dislodge the bitch off his back. No matter how hard he tried, she was stuck to him. He was going to get her if it was the last thing he did, the fucking cunt. Dirk McBride did not get treated this way.

"Get your fat ass off me or so help me, I will kill you." She laughed and he felt his anger get hotter. "Fucking cunt, get off—"

His head hit the floor. Blood erupted form his nose, and he nearly passed out when she did it several more times. Each time his forehead touched the floor, she would ask him if he was ready to leave in a voice that was calm and soft, sexy almost. And each time his answer was to call her names. When he started getting dizzy, he finally told her he was finished.

When she was off his back, Dirk turned on his back and jumped for her. He found himself sailing through the air before he even cleared the floor. The man was holding him up by his hair and his pants, and no matter how hard he tried, Dirk couldn't get away. After he was tossed into the yard, he reached for his gun.

It was gone. Dirk was ready to go back and get it, but the man on the steps made him pause. It was the asshole from the other morning, the one he'd hit. And the man, Mason, again had his gun. As much as he hated the things, he'd figured one might come in handy around here. But it only worked, he supposed, when he was the one holding it.

"You come back for more, Mason? And tell me, how did you enter my house? The front door again?" Mason only laughed at him as he handed the gun to his dad. "Give me that and I'll show you what it means to treat Dirk McBride like a commoner. Come on, Mason, you're not afraid that I'll shoot you, are you? Give me the fucking gun, Dad."

"I don't think so. I think I'll keep it until you grow up. And you're not coming back in here, Dirk. I already told you that."

Dirk was pissed and getting more so all the time. When he took the necessary steps to get to the wrap-around porch and to his dad, Mason stepped in front of him. "Get the fuck out of my way, Douglas. I'm going inside."

"Your father said you're not. And the last time I looked, his name was on the deed." Dirk tried to get around the big man. "You're not coming in here. Not while I'm still breathing, you're not."

"Then give me my gun and I'll take care of that little problem right now." Dirk fully expected him to hand it over. No one would dare to refuse him, and yet here they stood doing it. "You heard me. And what the hell are you doing in my house anyway? I thought I made it perfectly clear this morning that you're not to use the front door when you come to work for my dad."

"That was the day before yesterday, you moron. And I don't take orders from little pieces of shit that think they're all that. And for the record, you're nothing but a spoiled brat." Dirk had had enough. When he looked at his dad, Mason spoke again. "He's had it with you as well. And I don't think he's going to let you in either."

"Mom." Dirk shouted twice for his mom, and she came around the corner and stood on the porch with Dad. Dirk had had enough of these people and their supposed rules. He was a McBride, the Dirk McBride, and he was to be treated better than this. Especially by lower life forms like Mason. "Mom, don't let them do this to me. You know that this is not the way I deserve to be treated. Tell Dad that this is enough and to let me in. I'm not going to survive on the streets and you know it. I don't even have any cash on me."

"You don't have any credit cards either, son." Dirk looked at his dad when his mom spoke, her voice as hard and cold as he'd ever heard from her. "You're on your own. We've decided that you're too costly to have living here. If you get yourself straightened out and get some help, we'll think about—"

"Straightened out from what?" Neither of them answered him. "I swear to Christ, if this is one of those fucking intervention things, you're wasting my time. I'm not hurting anyone with my fun. And it's not like you can't afford to bail me out once in a while. I'm Dirk McBride."

"One hundred and seventy-three thousand, four hundred and fifty dollars." He asked his dad what that was. "What we've bailed you out with in the last six months. I'm afraid to look at what we've done for you since you've turned eighteen."

"So?" His parents looked at each other and then back at him. "So what if that's what it cost you? I'm your son, and you have the money. Fuck, if you'd just give me what's mine, then I'd not bother you at all. I think I'm old enough to have my inheritance now. And kicking me out isn't going to make a bit of difference except for when I get back in the house. You'll see what happens when you treat me this way."

"There is nothing left for you." Dirk just stared at his dad. "So far as I'm concerned, you spent your share of the inheritance from us a long time ago. Pain and suffering, money to bail you out. That's not even counting what Emma has given you or done for you. I'm washing my hands of you and what you think we owe you. Dirk, you're not going to do this to any of us any longer."

"She's a fucking lawyer. She should help me out. Did you forget who I am? What I represent to this family and the McBride name? Christ, just fucking get out of my way and let me in." Dirk tried again to move around Mason, and when that didn't work, he glared at his mom. "So this is how you're going to treat me? Just kick me away as if I mean nothing at all to you? This is how you treat your son? What the hell am I supposed to do about the money I owe to my friends? You think they have that kind of money to just piss away? There is thousands of dollars that I owe them. Look, just give me some money...I could use about ten grand. That should be a nice start if you're kicking me out. Then say, I don't know, you're going to have to give me about that much every month or I'll never have anything. What do you expect me to do if you just cut me off?"

Mason laughed. "Get a job? Save your money? Stop borrowing what your ass can't afford? I don't know, Dirk, those are just a few of the things you're going to have to figure out."

He lunged at the man and was knocked back on his ass just as the police pulled in the drive. Now things were going to get better for him. Turning to the cop as he got out of the car, Dirk started to explain what his family was doing to him, but the cop only cut him off.

"I'm afraid you're going to have to move on, Mr. McBride." It took Dirk a few seconds to realize that he was talking to him, not his dad. "You're trespassing as of right now. And it's well within my rights to arrest you for it."

"This is my house." The cop only shook his head and told him to move along. "I'm not going anywhere. These people are full of shit if they think I will. I'm fucking Dirk McBride. This is my home."

"Mr. McBride, I've called for backup, and if you don't get on down the road, we're going to take you to jail. Your parents filed for a restraining order against you this morning, and it has been granted. You're not welcome here anymore."

A second and third cruiser pulled in behind the first one. Dirk was pissed, but he wasn't stupid enough to think he could outrun a bullet should these idiots try and shoot him. Looking at the people on the porch, he just glared at them, then spit at Mason.

"You're going to regret this. All of you. I'm not going to be tossed away from here, my home. You'll see...I'm coming back, and when I do, you're going to wish you'd been better to me."

Mason came off the porch and stood within an inch of him. Dirk wanted to back up more, but he was leaning backwards over the cruiser as it was. Mason looked...well, like an animal, and Dirk was suddenly not just afraid of him, but scared shitless.

"You come back here and I will kill you," he said so only Dirk could hear. Mason's voice was hard and sounded like he meant it. "Come near any of them, especially my sister-in-law, and they'll never find you when I'm finished with you. Understand?"

"Fuck you."

Dirk turned and left them then. He had no idea what he was going to do, where he was going to go, but he had to leave or be hurt. Mason would hurt him. The man was bigger and stronger because he was nothing but a farm hand...one that was going to pay for treating Dirk McBride like he was nothing.

But not if I hurt Mason first, he thought. Dirk walked all the way to town, a cruiser right behind him the entire time. He had a plan by the time he found himself outside the bar he'd been at until closing time this morning. He was going to start him a tab and have it sent to his dad. That was the first part of his plan, and he loved it.

CHAPTER 4

Mason watched the cruiser. He didn't expect anything to happen right now, but he knew that this was just the beginning. When he heard the door to the house open then close, he turned to see who might be left. Landon was just sitting in one of the many rockers that sat on the big porch. Mason went to join him when he waved him over.

"I'm so embarrassed." Mason asked his friend why. "I never…I wasn't aware that Dirk was like this. So, he's so angry and…well, I hate to admit it, but I've been avoiding his temper in favor of giving in instead of just making him mind. Should have beaten him more as a child. But I'm glad you were here. I'd hate to think what might have happened if you hadn't been."

Mason laughed, and so did Landon. It was sad sounding coming from the elderly man, but Mason thought it made him feel less embarrassed. Things were settled enough between the two of them that Mason thought he could talk plainly with him. This was going to be hard, a very hard conversation to have, but he wanted him to be aware of what might happen now. But Landon spoke before he did.

"I'm not sure how to...you're not human, are you, Mason?" Mason told him he wasn't. "Yeah, I didn't think so. I suppose I should have asked you a while back, but there didn't seem to be any reason to. I know that Fox isn't either, and a few other men that work for me. Women too, I guess, but I never really cared so long as they didn't hurt me or my family."

"They won't. And they'll protect you in ways you cannot imagine. You didn't ask, but I'm a cougar, as is the rest of my family. Holly included, as of recently." Landon rocked in his chair for a few minutes before either of them spoke. "Landon, he's going to come back here. And when he does, it's not going to be just talking. He's going to try and hurt one or all of you."

"I know. Sad too, but...well, the only way I can see to have this solved is to just keep doing what we're doing. He's not right in the head if he thinks that over a hundred and seventy thousand dollars isn't worth being upset over." Landon rocked a little more. "He'll go after the weakest first. Right now, that will be my wife or daughter. I don't doubt that Emma can take care of herself, but right now her brother will take advantage of her being banged up."

"He'll go after your herd." Landon stopped rocking and looked at him. "They're your weakest point of entry. He'll kill them, poison the herd, and devastate this ranch. It might not bring you down money-wise, but it will hurt you. And ultimately, that's what he wants to do, hurt you."

"Maybe, but...nah, not the herd. That's what makes him the money that he's so free with. He might be a bastard, but he won't go after them. It'll be my family. I'll put out more patrols on the herd but.... Can you help me?" Mason nodded. "I mean, help me. I don't mean keeping an eye on him or just making sure that he doesn't hurt us. I mean help me get him straightened out."

"I'll hurt him." Landon nodded. "Landon, I'm a cougar, not a nice businessman that you can call up and say take his credit cards from him. To straighten him out, it might mean my cat taking him on."

"Whatever it takes." Landon stood up. "Come on in the house. I want you to meet my daughter, Emma. She's just made partner at her law firm. Kinda beat to crap, but she's the only thing I'm proud of right now."

Mason stood up. He knew what Landon was asking him. But he wasn't sure if Landon knew. If he hurt this family, if Dirk tried the shit on them—and Mason knew he would—then hell would be paid. As much as he liked this man, he disliked his son.

The house was a ranch style home, like most of the houses in this area. The only one with more than one level that he knew of was his brother's new house, and it was flipping huge in comparison. Even though Mason had never been in this house beyond the kitchen area, he knew that it was a sprawling home, with main rooms in the front and two sections or wings that came off each end to form around a large courtyard. He could see it when he was running or while he was out running fences.

He entered the main part and took off his hat. Fox was standing there waiting for him.

"Mr. Mason, I should like a word with you before you leave today." Mason nodded and Fox looked relieved. "My wife has baked you some cookies to take to your aunt as well. She bakes when she's nervous."

"She has a lot to be nervous about, I'm thinking." Fox nodded and handed him a beer. "Thanks. Do you suppose that Landon has any idea what his son is capable of?"

"No, sir, I do not." Mason nodded and looked into the room beyond. "Sir, this family means a great deal to us. I don't want anything to happen to them."

"Neither do I." Mason looked at Fox. "He wants me to buy his ranch. I can't, but he said he'd like for me to have it. I'd like nothing better than to do it, but it's way out of my price range. You think...do you think I'd be as good as him? I have no idea why I need to know that, but it would be nice to...I don't know...."

"I do, sir. I very much think you'd do very well." Handing Fox back the still full bottle, Mason took a deep breath. "You are a good man, Mason, much like your father."

Nodding, Mason entered the living room. He'd meet the daughter, then go on home. He had his own ranch to see to.

One look at the room and he stood there, stunned. Good Christ, it wasn't at all what he had expected. And then he looked at the woman on the couch.

Holly was sitting next to her, and Katie was on the other side of Emma. Mason moved into the room and stopped when Holly stood up. She looked...well, he was going to say fierce, but that wasn't quite right either.

"Mason?" He looked at her, only just realizing that he was staring at Emma. "Mason, you're scaring her. Take a step back."

"I have to talk to her. I need to touch her." Holly nodded but didn't move. "I need to...Holly, you need to help me."

"I don't think I can." The scent, the fear, and the smell of Emma was making his cat wild. He knew that he was scaring her—hell, he was scared himself—but he didn't move back until someone pulled him back. He growled low

54

and looked at Fox, who was talking to him, but Mason couldn't hear or even understand what he was saying. "She's my mate. And hurt."

"I understand that, sir, but you're making her mad. Look." Mason turned to look at Emma, and she was indeed pissed. When she stood up, her body lean and tall, he reached for her, only to have her slap his hands away.

"What the hell is wrong with you?" He had no answer for her other than he wanted to kill the men who had hurt her. "Are you addled? Do you need something cold to drink or something?"

"You." She moved back from him, and he growled. "You're mine. I need to...you're my mate."

"Mate?" Emma looked around the room and then back at him. "You need to explain yourself before I have you thrown from this house. And unlike my brother, I will hurt you because I'm not afraid to get myself dirty to do it."

"I'm not leaving you." His voice had gone hard. Mason's cat was pissed off that she was talking to them this way, and Mason was having a hard time controlling him. "You're my mate and hurt. I have to stay here, and...I have no idea, but I can't leave you like this."

"Mason?" He looked at Landon, who was standing between him and his mate now. "Mason, is she the one? Is Emma your mate? Truly?"

"Yes." He tried to calm himself too, but all he wanted was to touch Emma. "I can't...I'm not able to control the cat in me."

"Cat?" He looked at Emma. "Dad, what the hell is going on? What is wrong with him? Did Dirk hurt him?"

The low growl was all the warning he got. His cat didn't just take him, but seemed to consume him. He hurt from such a quick change. His cat didn't care and moved closer to his mate. When he was close enough to touch her, she fell back against the couch and moaned. He could hear Fox and Holly talking, but all he could see was Emma.

"Let him touch you." Emma looked up at Holly when she spoke. "He won't hurt you. He can't. But just let him touch you, all right?"

"He's a cat. A cougar. A big fucking cougar." Holly laughed and Emma turned to her, her eyes snapping. "Maybe this is old news to you, but I've never known a man that could just become something like...fuck, he's a cat."

"You know other shifters though, don't you, miss?" This was a question from Fox. "You just put out your hand and it will go a long way to calming the beast in him. He cannot hurt you, not ever. Just touch him."

Mason moved closer but not enough to touch her yet. The cat was in complete control right now, and he was afraid that he'd hurt her without meaning to. But when her hand came out slowly, he moved his big head to her and purred when she touched him.

Her fingers curled into his fur. His cat was moving closer to her when she jerked his head up. The snarl that came from him was cut off when she slapped him on the nose. His cat snarled again and was slapped harder this time.

"You listen here, you overgrown barn cat. I will not have you terrorizing me again, do you understand? This might be what you do in your home, but not in mine." The cat whimpered and Mason smiled inside. "What did you think was going to happen when this man comes into my parents' home and starts acting like...well, a fucking animal? Then you do this changing thing that, frankly, makes me want to find a gun and shoot you with it. Are you able to understand me?"

"If you let him taste you, then he can talk to you mentally." All sorts of ways to taste Emma came to mind, but he didn't move when Holly spoke. "I don't know if you have to actually draw blood to have a link...I'm still learning myself."

"You're a...well, of course, you are. You're married to one of his brothers, right?" Holly reminded Emma that she was pregnant too. "Congratulations. I think. I'm sorry, but this is a little too much for me. How do I get him to change back to a person? I have things I'd like to...discuss with the man here too."

"He'll be naked." Emma flushed brightly when her dad spoke, his voice full of humor. "This is better than I thought. Much...I dreamed of this, one of them boys being your husband, but well, this is the best news I've had all damned day."

"Landon, you're not helping." Katie came to stand near him and spoke to Fox next. "Take Mason to the kitchen, please, and see if you can find him something to pull on. I'm assuming you have something he can borrow?"

His cat didn't want to leave, but at least Emma wasn't throwing him out. Just before leaving, however, he put his head on her lap and stared up at her. She stared back at him, but he didn't think she was happy to have him there. Licking her arm, he went with Fox to the kitchen.

~~~

Emma stared at the fireplace. People were talking around her. They were more than likely talking to her, but she was still trying to wrap her mind around the fact that a man just turned into a cat in front of her.

It's not like she wasn't aware of shifters and other beings. Two of the men she worked with in the firm were wolves, and she was pretty sure that the man who cleaned up at night was a vampire. Not positive about that, but she was pretty sure. But not a one of them had turned in front of her. And now this man was saying she was his mate.

"What's a mate?" Everyone stopped talking when she asked. Almost embarrassed now to have interrupted them, she nearly told them to forget it. But Holly spoke first.

"The two of you are the other half of each other. You and Mason are destined to be together for the rest of your lives." Emma shook her head. "I'm sorry, but that's true. You can fight it—believe me, Jace did—but it won't work. And now that he's tasted your skin, he's going to be able to find you anywhere."

"And if I don't want this? How do I get this to not be…you know, us not to be mates?" No one answered her, and her mom just smiled. "This isn't funny. I have a life that I'm pretty happy with, and being a man's mate doesn't even figure into that for many years from now, if ever."

"I'm sure we can work something out." Mason entered the room pulling a shirt over his head. It, like the pants, was too big, but she didn't think that it distracted from his good looks in any way. "I'm sorry about my cat. He saw that you were hurt, and he needed to be near you."

"You have no control over him?" Her voice squeaked, but he only nodded his head. "You do have control, but not with me? That doesn't really make me all warm inside."

"Me either." Mason sat on the chair close to her and reached for her hand. She jerked it from him and he smiled. "We have to touch you, Emma. It's the only way that I can calm him. Just let me hold your hand for now and we can talk."

Emma turned to Holly to see if what he was saying was true, but only then realized they were alone. Fox entered then and set a tray down in front of her on the little table, but was in and out so quickly that she didn't get the chance to ask him anything. Turning to Mason, she glared at him when he took her hand again.

"This isn't going to work." He nodded but only kept grinning at her. "You're not...I don't even know you, and now you're saying that we're to be together for a while. This just doesn't happen in my world. Or anyone's, for that matter."

"Forever...not a little while, but forever." She didn't like the sound of that any more than she did "for a while," but didn't comment when he continued. "I'm a cougar, as you've seen first-hand. My parents are both gone as you might know, but my family and I have been what we are since birth. I'm not really...the only contact, real contact, I've had with a mate is my brother's mate. And you know Holly. We never...I guess we've been too busy trying to carve out a bit of our own earth to worry about what it is to have a mate."

"She said she's going to have a baby. Holly did, she said she was pregnant." Mason nodded. "Could you stop doing that and speak to me? I hate bobbers, and you're making me insane with it."

"All right. Yes. Holly is going to have a baby. It'll be a child just like you were when you were born, in case you wondered, but when it turns about twenty-five, he'll be able to shift. Had Holly been a cat from birth, the baby would be able to shift sooner. It still might. We're waiting to see when it's born. You should eat."

The abrupt change of subject threw her off, so when he handed her the sandwich on a plate, she took it without thinking. It made him let go of her hand and for some reason she felt like she'd been smacked on the hand. Eating the sandwich, she thought it better than asking him to hold her again. Emma was as confused as she'd ever been about things.

"I'm sure you have questions. I do too. I'm not…there is a lot I don't know about mates either. We're all learning this as we go." Her mouth was full or she might have stopped him there. They were not going to be mates, not now or ever. "Our kind mates for life. If one of us dies, the other either dies too or raises the children, should there be any. But we breed fast too. And only with our mates."

"I don't want children. I have a job, a career to go back to when…what makes you think that we're really mates? I mean, this just could be wishful thinking on your part." He started to shake his head and then told her no, it wasn't wishful thinking. "Then what? Is there some sort of telltale, like in poker? Or do you just take on the weak and hope that someday they really are what you want?" Flushing, she knew that she'd been rude and told him that. But he only smiled.

"Can you stand without hurting?" She put the plate down and asked him why. "You wanted to know and I'm going to show you. I could more than likely explain it, but you're not going to believe that either."

Standing up cost her; Emma was sore and hurting still. Her wrist was in a sling, but the pain pills seemed to keep that pain at bay. But she'd had a chance to see herself in the mirror this morning and she'd realized how lucky she really was to be alive.

"I'm going to touch you." She was afraid to speak. He was so close she could smell his cologne, and wondered what it was he wore. Mason also smelled of leather, old and worn, the earth, and something else. "Don't move. If you do, my cat is going to think you're not okay with what I'm doing."

"What is it you're going to do?" Instead of answering her, he put his face in her neck. Her entire body seemed to come alive. Well, not just alive, but "mother fuck I've just put my finger in an electrical socket" alive.

His breath was warm, almost hot as it touched her throat. Her pulse seemed to pick up in speed, and she wanted to hold onto something. *Mason*, her mind screamed, *hold onto Mason*. The smell was stronger now, almost too much, but really not enough either. When he put his hands on her waist, gently, and pulled her to him, his cock touched her pussy and she moaned.

She felt him stretch and harden, and she wanted more of him. When he rocked into her, it took her breath away and she put her hand on his shoulder. It was that or tumble back on the couch with him on top of her.

"Do you feel it?" She nodded and found herself seeking his neck. When she was there, she wanted to taste his flesh, lick him and see if he tasted as good as he smelled to her. "You have a scent that only I can smell. A taste that only I can taste. Our love making will be fast, hard, and consuming. You'll come so many times that exhaustion will take you, only to wake and want it again and again."

When he rocked into her again, she felt her body respond. The need to come with this man was making her mouth water, and when he pulled her closer still, she nipped at his pounding pulse and moaned. Need hurt her, it was so strong. Her clothing was too tight and too heavy. Her nipples needed to be freed, suckled, and then bitten. Her body was no longer hers but his, and she wanted him to have it now.

"I've never felt this way before. I want you to take me right here. This is…is this right?" She waited for him to laugh at her, but he moved her head so that he could bury his mouth over her throat. The need for him to bite her was making her wetter. Her pussy felt tight and ready for him. Wrapping her leg around him, around his hip, had him lifting her from the floor. "Take me. Please. I need to come with you."

"I can't." Her heart hurt at his words, but he took her mouth and kissed her with the desperation that she was feeling. "I want you. Christ, do I want you. But I can't take you here. Your family is just in the other room. But I need to mark you."

Anything, she thought, *just do something that will make me feel whole.* Mason kissed her again, his mouth doing things to hers that she knew he wanted to do to her body. Hell, she wanted him to do the things to her. When he moved along her chin to her throat again, she nearly cried out when he sucked her flesh into his mouth. Her body was suddenly pressed against a wall with him rocking hard into her.

"I'm going to bite you." Nodding, she started to beg him to take her somewhere and do whatever he wanted, but she was so close now that if he stopped she was going to scream. "Come for me, Emma. Let me taste you when you come."

"Please."

His mouth seemed to be everywhere. His hands were cupping her breast hard over her blouse. The pinch to her nipple had her looking down to find his dark hand cupping her bare breast and tugging at her nipple. When he leaned down and took the hard tip into his mouth, she cried out again, this time with a small hard punch of a climax. When he lifted his head and looked down at her, she nearly begged him to finish her, but she didn't have to worry. He watched her face while he fucked her hard through their clothing.

"Come."

Her body seemed to know that he was boss. And when she cried out this time, his body bowing back from the wall, he put his hand over her mouth and bit deeply into her throat.

Her body screamed out a release, and before she was finished, a second then a third one left her weak, yet needing more. He suckled at her throat, his hands still at her breast, when he lifted his head suddenly and kissed her. She wanted more…her spent body seemed to need more. And when he brought her again, giving her another mind-blowing climax, she went limp in his arms while he held her.

Emma held onto him. He was speaking, but she was too fuzzy, too everything to listen to him. No one had ever made her feel this way during sex. She was lucky if she got any enjoyment out of it at all, and this man had given her so much. Trying to listen to him, she realized that he was telling her he was sorry, and she lifted his head up by his hair.

"You should know that instead of finding that painful, it's very sexy to me." Emma jerked his hair harder. "Okay, that, not so much. Would you like for me to have you hold me this way near your pussy? The thought of eating you has me hard as stone."

To prove his point, he rocked into her again. Moaning, she could feel another climax building and wanted it in the worse kind of way. She looked at the man giving her this, making her feel this way, and asked him to stop. He did, much to her body's dismay.

"What have we done?" He put his face back into her neck, and she felt his hot tongue roll over her skin. She nearly begged him to make her come again, but he lifted his head and took her to the couch. When she was seated, he stood by the fireplace, about as far from her as he could get. "Are you mad? Because I have to tell you, that's the best sort of sex I've ever had. And if you ever want to do it again I'm here...but I'm thinking it was more than that. Wasn't it?"

"We're bonded. Not mated yet—that would require us to bite each other during a climax—but we're about there now." She felt her body respond to his words, and it wasn't as scary as she'd hoped it would be. *I can talk to you through a link now. You can...I think you can me as well, but I'm not sure.*

His voice was gentle in her head, almost like he was really talking to her. But she had no idea if she was ready to talk to him that way, and ignored the ease with which he'd made the connection to her.

"And this need? This overwhelming need to be fucked by you, it's this mate thing?" He nodded and she wanted to ask more, but wasn't really sure how to begin. "Did you know that it was going to happen between us? I mean, my dad is thrilled, like he's been planning this...you didn't do this to get the ranch, did you? You're no better than my brother if you did. I'll have you know right now that—"

She found herself on her back. He was over her and pressing his body into hers. Instead of pushing him off, which was what her head was telling her to do, she pulled him down to her mouth and kissed him, telling him with her body how much she needed him. But when he lifted his body from hers and stood over her, Emma whimpered, her body aching to have his.

"I'm leaving now before we do something that we'll regret." Emma sat up, her face level with his hard cock outlined in his jeans. "If you keep looking at me like that, Emma, I'm going to bend you over this couch and fuck you like the animal you just accused me of being."

With that, he turned and left her. The door closing to the room she was in was loud to her, ringing of an anger that she was beginning to feel herself. How dare he leave her without explaining? Getting up, she went to find her father. If he had done this to her, she was going back home and never returning. She might anyway.

CHAPTER 5

Zach watched Mason. Whatever demon he was trying to get rid of wasn't going away any time too soon. When the hammer he was using broke in half, Mason threw it across the field and looked like he was going to toss something else when he turned to him.

"You do and you'll walk funny for the rest of your life. And that mate of yours, whoever she is, is going to be very disappointed in you too." Mason growled and Zach laughed. "That bad, huh? Who is she? The Mitchell girl? I heard she was in town. Or is it someone else?"

"Emma McBride." Zach had no idea who she was but nodded. "She's got this brother, Dirk, who I want to—"

"Wait. Dirk the Dick's sister? You're mated to Dirk the Dick's sister?" Zach started laughing, and even when Mason had him pinned to the fence post they were setting, it didn't stop him from laughing harder. "Christ man, is she as bad as him?"

"No. Christ." Zach was dropped to the ground, but since he didn't think Mason was satisfied, he stayed where he was. As funny as he found this, he didn't think Mason was in a mood to fuck with. Well, maybe a little bit, but not enough to get the shit knocked out of him. "She's beautiful and sexy. Smart too. I guess she's a partner in a law firm in the city. Mother fuck."

Zach stopped laughing when he realized how hurt his brother was. "Did she say something to you? Is she, I don't know, pissed that you're mated with her?"

"No. That's not a problem. But her dad...for months now her dad has been hinting that I buy him out. And a couple of mornings ago he told me that I should marry his daughter and I could have the entire ranch free and clear. I can't buy him out, and now...Christ now, it seems that his daughter will be marrying me and we'll have the farm anyway." Zach asked him if she knew that part. "Not yet, but knowing her dad, he's more than likely telling her how this was his plan all along and that he was going to have grandkids. Then this shit with her brother came up."

Zach listened while Mason told him what had happened with Dirk the Dick. He really wasn't surprised by the news. Dirk had been a prick since he'd known him. And he was forever telling everyone that he was too rich to be stuck here. He'd even bragged how he had anything he'd wanted whenever he wanted all the time. Zach had always blamed his parents until he met Katie and Landon a few years ago. Then he realized it was just Dirk. A pig-headed asshole.

If there were any nicer people in the world than the McBrides, he didn't believe it. Katie was kind and giving, her husband loud and boisterous. Funny, both of them were, and you could tell that they loved each other like they were pack and not humans. Zach always thought that his parents were like them, kind and loving and needing each other.

"What are you going to do about him?" Mason didn't answer but looked out over the field that separated their ranch from two others. "Do you think he'll come back there? I did notice that there were more wolves around."

"I do think he'll come back. And when he does, he's going to do some major damage to them. Not just the property and land, but to them as well. I don't think that Landon is really aware of how much one man can do to them." Mason tuned to him then. "I had to go back and talk to Fox. He's been keeping tabs on Dirk. The boy has been in more trouble in the last month than all of us put together over our lifetimes. He throws these elaborate parties, then trashes the hotel that he has them in. There have been three wrecks with his car that have caused more damage than we owe on everything we have. And Fox said that it happens weekly. Things that a man his age should have outgrown by now, but he acts like he is owed it. Last month he trashed a hotel room and cost Landon nearly ten grand to fix it back. And when asked about it, Dirk told him to fuck off. Had we talked to our parents that way...hell, even Aunt Georgie...we would be picking ourselves up in another state."

That was true. Zach remembered when he'd been ten and decided that he wanted to try cursing. He wasn't any good at it, but he'd picked up a few words that he thought he'd like to add to his vocabulary. They were a wrong choice, and Aunt Georgie had shown him the error of his ways very harshly. Zach had been very careful of his words when he'd been around his aunt since then.

"So now what? You can't just leave her there to be hurt by him. And from your...mood, I can tell that the two of you didn't part ways on a good note." Mason just growled. "Yeah, that's going to work with her. Tell me what you want me to do to help you. Not with her...I'm as clueless as you are about mates and stuff, but I can see what I can find out about Dirk."

"He's been put out. Landon has had him taken out of the will, the locks have been changed on the house, and he has no car or money. Credit cards have been cancelled, as well as his access to the bank has been taken out. I talked to Fox and he's going to remind Landon to call all the merchants in town and tell them that if Dirk charges anything, damages anything, then he's responsible for it." Zach was impressed, but they both knew that changing the locks and the other things was only going to make him madder. He told Mason that too. "Yeah, I know that, but I don't think Landon gets it. I think he thinks his son will come back to him with open arms after he sees what it's like to have nothing and to have to fend for himself."

Dirk would blame this all on his family and never see that all of it was his doing. Zach knew this, and he was pretty sure that Mason did as well. The man was bad news, and there was little you could do to someone like that short of killing them. And Zach had a feeling it might just come to that.

Mason went to the truck and got another post and a hammer. This one would stand more because Mason seemed to be, while not better, in a lighter mood. The two of them planted three more posts before Mason spoke again.

"I'm having some of the wolf pack nearby patrol the grounds, as you noticed. Mackley said he'd do it, but it would cost me. He knew that I'd mated with Emma and wants to be able to run on the property some. I told him I'd have to talk to her, and he thought that smart." Zach had to agree. He'd noticed that things went better for Jace when he included his wife in things. "I have no idea what to do with her."

"What do you mean, do with her? And if I were you, I'd never say that in front of Holly. It might get you castrated." They both laughed. "Just love her, I guess. What comes will come. I'm thinking that sooner or later this thing with Dirk is going to come to a head, and he'll either straighten up or be killed. I'm thinking, from my own experience with the man, that he'll be dead long before he gets a clue."

By nightfall they had planted nineteen posts. Tomorrow, Gerard would deliver the fencing that they'd ordered and Darin and Logan would start to put it up. That was a four-man job, and he and Mason would help them as soon as they put in the rest of the posts. Ranching was hard work, but Zach loved it.

~~~

Dirk had nowhere to go. And not only that, he didn't have a dime on him. Going to the bank had left him pissed off and nearly put in jail, but he'd managed to get out of that too. Fuck, this shit was getting old. And now his fucking phone wasn't working.

"Dad, you're going to regret this." Dirk sat down at the table at the diner and tried to think how he was going to get the woman behind the counter to give him some food. The last two places he'd been to, trying to order and charge it to his dad, hadn't worked and he really didn't expect it to here. When the woman brought him a glass of water and no menu, he figured she'd been called too.

There were crackers on the table, and he reached for a handful of them before those too were snatched away. He wanted to toss them back in the waitress's face and tell her to fuck off, but he might not have anything to eat again for however long his dad was in a snit. And then there was Mason.

That guy was really going to get it for making his dad do this, because Dirk had no doubt that it was all Mason's doing and not his dad's. First of all, his parents weren't that smart, and even if Emma had suggested it, they'd never do this to their only son. Especially him. Dirk was a god to his family and they seemed to have forgotten that since Mason had been sniffing around his land. And even though he'd told his dad he wanted no part of ranching, he certainly didn't want Mason to have any of it.

The cop sitting down across from him made Dirk sit up. He wasn't afraid of him but thought about tearing him apart for assuming that he could sit with him, Dirk McBride. But the man spoke before he could say anything.

"You have any money?" Dirk told him he was worth billions. "Nah, that's what your daddy is worth. Do you have any money on you?"

"You know I don't. What did my father do, call you up and tell you to come looking for me? Well, you can take a message back to him for me. Tell him this has gone on long enough and for him to call off his dogs. I'm sick of him thinking he can teach me a lesson." The cop just leaned back and let the waitress put the biggest fucking burger with fries in front of him. Then when she set down a thick milk shake — strawberry, his favorite — Dirk started to reach for it. As far as he was concerned, and it had been that way his entire life, everything was his if Dirk McBride wanted it. But the slap to his face had him nearly hitting back at the man.

"This is mine, you little shit." The man ate the burger like it was his last meal and he was going to savor every bite. He even moaned a few times while swallowing it down with a few fries. Dirk started to reach for it again, this time snagging a fry. As he shoved it in his mouth, Mason sat beside him. It suddenly became a lump in his throat.

"Hello, Dirk the Dick." Dirk couldn't even say anything around the knot of fry. "You and I are going to have a nice talk, and Howie LeBlanc here—the sheriff, if you didn't know it—is going to be my witness that I don't hurt you. Unless, of course, you are stupid. Then all bets are off."

Dirk drank down his water, trying to dislodge the wad that was cutting off his air. When his head hit the table, twice, he glared at Mason. The man had hit him so hard that he was sure a rib or two was broken.

"You motherfucker, that fucking hurt." Mason grinned and told him he was trying to help him from choking. "By giving me a concussion? I want you to know right now that when my dad gets over his snit about this shit, I'm going to make you pay. No one treats Dirk McBride this way and lives to tell about it."

"Your dad isn't dealing with you any longer. I am. And it's doubtful that you've ever hurt anyone with your fists, much less killed them. You're too much of a pussy." Mason leaned back and stared at him before he spoke again. "We're going to iron this out. Then you're going to be a good boy or I'm going to take great pleasure in showing you how we deal with shits like you."

"Christ. Do you have any idea who you're talking to? Do you know what's going to happen to you when my parents find out what you're doing? I'm Dirk McBride. My very name should make you tremble in your shoes."

Mason looked at the cop. LeBlanc stared at him for several seconds before they both started laughing, a loud guffawing kind of laughter that reminded him of braying jackasses.

Dirk jabbed his fist into Mason's face. His victory over what he'd done was short lived when he found himself with his face nearly being imbedded into the table top. Mason was holding him down with only one hand, and Dirk couldn't move.

"Listen to me, you little fuck. In a few weeks I'm going to marry your sister and we're going to take over the ranch, and all that entails. You come near her or any other member of my family — and that would include your parents — and I will hunt you down. And you'd better believe me when I tell you that I will hunt you down." Dirk started to speak, yell at the man, when his head hit the table three times in a row. His head felt as if it was going to explode and he was sure that his nose was broken. Blood stained the table. He could see it each time his head was lifted to be slammed back down. When his head was lifted again, Dirk braced himself for the pain when he was let go.

"You motherfucker. You're going to pay for this when my dad finds out how you treated me. And as for you marrying my sister? Not going to happen. I'll make sure it doesn't." Mason asked him how he thought he was going to do that. "Because I'm the heir apparent, you cock sucker, and what I say will carry a lot of weight regardless of what my dad is doing right now."

"You just don't get it, do you? You're not welcome back." Mason laid an envelope on the table. "Your dad sent you that. It's all you're going to get from him until you do the required steps that are listed on that contract. Until then, you are not to come near them, contact them, or have anything to do with the ranch or anything that is owned by either the Douglases or the McBrides."

"Contract?" Dirk reached for the envelope and opened it. Inside was a hundred dollars in twenties and a folded blue sheath of papers, plus a note. He pulled it out and read it before stuffing it all back in the envelope and tossing it on the table. "No. And hell no."

Neither man said anything to him. No one begged him to reconsider or even to look it over again. Taking napkins from the dispenser on the table, he cleaned up his nose and tossed the used napkins on the table. Still neither of them spoke. Dirk hated it, but he was not going to speak first if it killed him. After another ten minutes the waitress brought LeBlanc a refill on his tea and Mason a glass of iced tea. It was then that Dirk couldn't stand it any longer.

"I'm not going to do it no matter what you do to me." Mason shrugged and sipped his tea. LeBlanc just smiled as he ate his pie...apple it smelled like, with ice cream on it. "And how much more money am I going to get? Because that isn't going to take care of me for an hour. I need clothing, a hotel. Then I'll need to eat. I have plans for this...you know what, tell Dad that I'll take a thousand a week, and that should be enough until I get things arranged."

"There's nothing else. And I have a bag of clothing for you. Oh, and your credit cards are done too, in case you didn't know that. So is your access to the bank. The phone you have is no longer working, and you don't have any way to use the family vehicles. None of them." Dirk had figured out most of that on his own, but Mason continued. "Any bills you incur, any money that you owe from this day on will be your own responsibility. Trouble that you get into, with merchants or even the police, no one is going to bail you out of. As of the moment you left the ranch, you were an adult making it on your own in the world. If I were you, I'd take this as a learning lesson and stop acting like a spoiled little bitch."

"You think this makes me mad?" Dirk laughed. Even to him it sounded a little forced. But he was mad and he wanted this shit finished so that he could go back home. "I'm going to be back in my family home by the end of tomorrow, and you're going to be out on your ass so fast that you're not going to know what hit you. As for this shit, this pile of shit in that envelope, you can shove that up your ass right now. It is not going to happen."

"Your life." LeBlanc got up and went to the cash register. Mason stood as well and looked down at him. "You're a real piece of work, Dirk. And a great disappointment to your family. They're a really nice group of people, and here you are — what the fuck happened?"

"You think they're nice? I know that they love me and that soon, like I told you, this will be over and they'll never try to teach me a lesson again. But nice? No, I wouldn't call any of you nice after this. And you, you shit fuck, will be old news." Dirk stood as well and realized again just how tall this man was. "Back off, Mason, or I'm going to have you arrested for assault. I might just do that anyway."

"Yeah, good luck with that." He moved to the register and while his back was turned, Dirk snatched up the envelope. There was no way that he was going to do anything on that list, but he wanted the money. Until his parents came to their senses and let him come back home, he had to have some pocket money. He was nearly to the door when Mason said his name. A duffle was tossed at him and it nearly knocked him on his ass. "Good luck. Oh, and stay off the ranch, Dirk. I've put some patrols on, and you won't want to fuck with them."

Dirk went out into the night. He'd not realized how cold it had gotten, and now he wished he had a coat. Thinking there might be one in the bag, he leaned against the wall and opened it. Maybe his parents had given him more in the bag and not told Mason. Whatever he had over them, Dirk knew that they'd help him if they could. Mason had a lot to pay for when he returned home soon.

There were five shirts, not even his best ones. Three pair of pants, again ones that he didn't care for. His mom should have let him pick them, but then had he been there, this travesty wouldn't be necessary. There were underwear, socks, and some undershirts. In the pockets on the outside was a bathroom kit filled with shampoo, toothbrush, and some paste, deodorant, and a few other things like mouth wash and some soap. It was a bar, not the kind he always used, no loofa, and there wasn't even any lotion for his arms and legs when he got out of the shower. Someone should have known that he'd need these items and provided them for him. Or at least money so he could go and get them. The number of things that Mason was going to pay for was mounting. Dropping the items that were beneath him to the ground, he dug into the rest of the bag, even dumping everything on the ground to see if there was a hidden pocket or a zipper that he'd missed. Nothing.

When he screamed out his frustrations, several people turned to look at him. "What the fuck are you looking at? Huh? I'm being treated like I fucking don't matter, and it's all his fault." One man simply told him it was about time, and a woman with children told him to behave in public. When he made like he was going to lunge at her, she simply flipped him off and moved on. Dirk started to leave the shit there, and decided that he'd check the pockets of his clothing first. But now he had to find a place to sleep.

Gathering everything up, including the shit he wasn't ever going to use, he stuffed it in the bag. He'd missed something...that was all. There was no way that his mom or dad would treat him this way. By the time he found a hotel, he knew what was going on.

Mason had knocked his sister up. That would be the only reason that his family would allow such a lowlife as him to be near his family. And kicking him, Dirk McBride, out was a way to keep him from hurting Mason for having the nerve to soil his sister. Emma was all right when he needed her, but for the most part she irritated him to no end. She had told him he was on his own from now on, and the one time he'd called her since, she'd told him she was too busy to deal with him. It was all Mason, all of this shit was Mason, and he was going to pay.

It took him nearly three more hours to find a place to sleep. The first one had tried to run his credit card and had cut it up in front of him. Like that was going to solve his problem. The next time he went to a hotel, it was one that demanded that he put up a deposit. That argument had nearly gotten him arrested. Dirk was nearly down the street when he remembered the hotel and a previous experience there.

"Shitty place I'd never even take my dog." He'd had a party there one night recently and they had gotten nasty with him over the noise. He'd shown them. The room looked like a bomb had exploded in it when he'd left. Dirk remembered his dad and mom saying something about the cost of his stay, but he hadn't paid any attention. "Like money means anything to you when you have it all."

Walking on until he was in the worst part of town, Dirk ended up in a hotel room that was smaller than his closet. It was the best he could afford after giving the man a nice shirt. He'd have to talk to his mom about giving him more money. She'd be the one to talk to. His dad was too into Mason to listen to him right now. A hundred a day wasn't going to cut it. Dirk wished now he'd of remembered to ask him where the next allotment was going to be and when.

"Can't be too early. I need my beauty rest." He lay on the lumpy bed and then got up and found a notepad and pen left in the room by the hotel. He headed the paper with the word "NEEDS" and started writing down the things he felt that he should have while in exile.

"First and foremost I need my credit cards back. Money is important to a man like Dirk McBride, and not having it is really cramping my style. I need to be seen and seen looking good." He went on to add things like a car, nicer clothing, as well as some cash. It had taken him a second list to figure out how much he needed to have on him at all times, and figured that if they just set it up so he could have a grand a day, he'd let them know how much more he'd need at the end of the week.

Calling his parents to find out a few things that Mason had neglected to tell him had proven harder than he'd wanted to mess with. They weren't listed in the phone book, his sister only had a cell phone, and the stupid bitch at the information number he'd been told to call wouldn't give it to him...something about her not having a listing. Emma always listed her phone number in case someone needed her. Like him.

Yawning, he ordered a pizza and was really pissed that they told him they didn't deliver to where he was. He was told he'd have to call someone closer to where he was to get it delivered, but if he wanted to come and pick it up, they'd need a credit card to start his order.

"I'm Dirk McBride." The person on the other end of the phone said nothing. "Did you hear me? I'm Dirk McBride. I have the ranch out near the Collin River."

"Doesn't mean anything to me, buddy. Maybe you should call someone who cares."

The phone went dead in his hand. Dirk felt his temper, always right there on the edge, let go, and he jerked the phone out of the wall. Thinking of the shit his parents were needlessly putting him through, he trashed the entire room before falling on the broken bed in an exhausted sleep. That'll teach them, he thought with a smile, and fell asleep.

CHAPTER 6

Emma woke in her bed, not remembering where she was for several seconds. Home. She was home and on a mandatory leave. Getting up, she went to the bathroom and turned on the shower and looked at herself in the mirror. The woman staring back at her wasn't the same as the one she'd seen when she'd gotten up yesterday.

The bruises were all gone. Not just gone, but like they'd never been there. There wasn't even a light brownish yellow tint to her cheek, and the cut on her lip was gone too. Looking down at her arm, thinking that she might not want to look at it again after yesterday, she stared at it for several seconds before she felt a slight vibration in her head.

Good morning. Staggering back from the sink and mirror, she stood there while Mason laughed in her head. But that was silly. How could he be in her head? *It is me. I can speak to you this way; remember me telling you that?*

"I don't want to talk to you this way." Waiting for him to answer her when she'd spoken aloud, she tried again, speaking to him the way he had her. *I don't want to talk to you at all, but this way is out of the question.*

You're scared. Was she? Emma supposed that she had been. Now, however, she was mad. *And now you're pissed. I'm just concerned, that's all. Your brother has caused some damage to the hotel here in town, and I wondered if he'd contacted you about it.*

Her parents had sat her down last night and told her everything. Dirk, it seemed, had been doing things, a great many things, that had caused her mom and dad a lot of pain and embarrassment. Not just financially, but he'd also hurt them with his complete lack of care as to what he did or how it affected the people around him. They'd also told her what they were doing to him in hopes that it would bring him around. Emma hadn't told them, but she thought it was too late for her brother to ever have a redeemable quality about him. In turn, she told them what she'd been doing for him and her last conversation with him. It seemed that they were all on the same page about Dirk.

I would like to talk to you today. She wanted him to leave her alone, but that wasn't going to happen either, she found out. *There are some things that I'd like to talk to you about, something I need to tell you, and I'd really like to know what you can tell me about your brother's habits, his friends, and whatever else you might know that can help us.*

Help us who? She waited for him to answer and stepped into the shower. Her arm, like her body, was healed. While Emma didn't know exactly how it had happened, she was willing to bet it had a great deal to do with the man talking to her. *You're not answering me.*

Holly isn't well this morning, and I'm talking to my brother too. She could not just hear the worry in his voice, but feel it too. It was as if his emotions were hers. *Can you just come over here, please? I...she's really sick. I know that Jace is taking her to the doctor, but I still worry. She's my sister.*

I'll be right there. Tell Jace to give her some crackers and tea. I'll have my mom make her some of the stuff she gives me when I'm sick. It's not going to hurt her or the baby. He told her he'd tell her. *Also, you healed me, didn't you?*

I did. She waited for him to tell her more, but he changed the subject again. *Are you in the shower?*

How the hell do you know that? His laughter did nothing to soothe her temper. *Are you spying on me? Do you have someone watching my every move? If you are, I want you to call them off right fucking now.*

I don't have anyone watching you, love. I can feel that you're aroused. She stopped cupping her breasts and tried to calm her body. *You're thinking of what I did to you yesterday. What we started. I'm telling you right now, my cock has been hard since I left you. And no amount of jerking off has helped. I need you.*

You masturbated without me? He moaned in her head and she cupped her breast again. *You gave me such wonderful releases yesterday. I can't help but think what it will be like when you take me. Not that you will, but it's a wonderful fantasy.*

I'd very much like to join you right now. I'd be down on my knees before you, sucking that pretty pussy of yours. Is your clit hard, Emma? Do you feel it when you slide your fingers into your heat? She was panting, her body on fire for the man she didn't care for. *Come for me, baby. I'm going to pull my cock free and join you. When you come, and I want you to, I want you to think of me coming all over the tree that's in front of me, hard and quick strokes to bring me when you come.*

Her fingers were busy in her pussy, her hands were all over her breasts, but it wasn't enough. Not nearly enough. When he told her that he was close, his balls were tight against his body, she pinched her clit hard as she tugged at her nipple. The climax nearly took her breath away, and when he cried out in her mind that he was coming too, that his cum was splashing all over the ground, she came again, her body bowed back in ecstasy.

Emma was leaning against the wall of the shower now. She was spent, but she really wanted more. The man in her head was telling her how much he wanted her now, how he'd like to do things to her that wasn't helping her right at the moment. When he asked her to come outside, to meet him at the well on the back end of her property, she jerked the water off and grabbed a towel, wondering if she had time to come again before she found him.

I'm hard for you. Come quickly. Not bothering with a bra or panties, she pulled a heavy sweatshirt over her head and was still tying off her sweatpants when she slipped her feet into her boots. Grabbing a coat off the hook as she went out the door, Emma was nearly to the well when she saw him. He was naked, his cock standing straight from his body, and all she could think about was tasting him.

Mason grabbed her up as soon as she leapt at him. Need was growing out of control, and she needed him to finish her. He pulled her shirt up and over her head and dropped it, and Emma cried out when he took her nipple into his mouth and bit her.

"Christ, I haven't thought of anything else but you." She moaned when he put his hands down the back of her pants and cupped her bare ass. "Baby, you're so wet I can almost taste you. And I want to. More than anything in this world, I want to feel you coming down my throat."

"Please. Eat me." She felt his low growl and then was set away from him. When he told her to lie down on her clothing, she did as he wanted. Spreading her legs wide for him, she slid her fingers into her pussy and played while he stood over her. His cock was hard, straining from his body, and he held himself in his fist as he watched her.

"I'm going to enjoy this." She told him she would as well. He dropped to his knees and her pussy gushed. She took it on her fingers and rubbed it all over her breasts before reaching for him. Mason fell on her, his mouth sucking her clit and biting down on it before she could touch him.

The climax ripped from her. Not a soft, gentle building, but a full out release. When he slid his fingers into her, touching her spot that few men had ever even tried to find, she came again, screaming out his name as she held him to her. Christ, she was going to die from this, and right now she couldn't have cared less as her body built again for what was going to no doubt be another amazing release.

He ate her, devoured her for so long that she felt like her body was no longer hers but his. When he stood up over her body, his cock was so thick and hard that she reached out and couldn't wrap her fingers around him. His precum was just enough to make her slide up and down his cock easily. Her need, however, only increased.

"I need to be inside of you." She nodded but didn't let him go. "Emma, if you keep that up, I'm going to come all over you and not inside of you where I desperately want to be."

"I want to taste you too." He moaned, leaning back so that she could touch him all she wanted, and she did. Taking only his crown into her mouth, she moaned when he held her to him, his big hand cupping the back of her head while he fucked her mouth hard.

Mason tasted like no man she'd ever tasted before. His cum was hot, not warm, and it was spicy, creamy, and thick as it slid over and in her mouth. When he told her he was close, too close to stop if she didn't stop now, Emma let him go and fisted him as he released, his cum spraying all over her face and breasts so that it felt as if he were branding her.

When she thought him finished, she leaned back and stared up at him. But he wasn't, and when he told her to stand up, he lifted her over him. Emma screamed when he slammed his hard thick cock into her, her body pressed against a tree. The pain and pleasure of it took her breath away. He was too much, yet not enough. Even as he fucked her, her legs wrapped around him to hold him, she felt his mouth at her breast and knew that he was going to bite her there. When he lifted his head, she looked into the darkest eyes she'd ever seen and knew that things were never going to be the same again.

"When you come, bite me." Shaking her head, he told her yes. "You have to mark me, Emma. Take my blood into your body so that we're one."

His cock was hitting her harder now. Each stroke was bringing her closer and closer to her release. This one, she knew, was going to be the best ever. And when he sank his teeth into her breast, she screamed out his name even as she bit deep into his throat. The taste took her breath away, and the feeling of it, unlike anything she'd ever felt, had her wanting more.

Blood filled her mouth. Like his cum, it was hot, but didn't have the coppery taste she'd always associated with blood. Instead, it tasted like honey, the best chocolate, and the finest wine in the world. Coming again, her body exploded with her release, and stars burst behind her eyelids even as blackness swallowed her.

~~~

Mason held her in his arms. For as much as he wanted to take her again, just holding her right now was enough. He looked down at her and realized how weak he was from his release. Mason went down on the ground and rolled to his back, taking her with him. The sweatshirt that she'd had on only covered her ass, but he held her to his warm body and hoped she was warm enough. Christ, it hit him suddenly, he had a mate.

Nothing could have prepared him for the emotions that were running through him at the moment. Not even the conversation he'd had with Jace last night had made him think that it would be this consuming. He had no idea what to do now, but first and foremost was to make her and to keep her happy. When she lifted her head and looked down at him, he could see a drop of blood on her lip and kissed her.

"This means something." He nodded, not sure of her tone. She wasn't mad, he didn't think, but she really wasn't happy either. "The sex, is it always going to be like this? So…I don't know, so wow."

"Wow? I guess that's as good a word as any. And I hope so. Christ, woman, you nearly killed me." Her grin had him kissing her nose. "I'm not the mushy type of man, but you are, simply put, the most amazing woman I've ever been with."

Her body stretched over his and his cock stirred to life. Emma stilled when he held her to him, and when she rolled her hips, he was as hard as he'd been before. She sat up over him, his cock still buried deeply within her, and started a slow, smooth ride.

"Sex has never been all that great with other men." Mason didn't point out that he'd rather not talk about other men with her, but he'd done the same thing earlier and was okay with it for now. "You're going to be the only one from now, I was told. My dad apparently knows a great deal about your kind. Not everything, he told me, but a lot."

"Yes. Shifters are very possessive and violent when it comes to their mate. Holly and Jace had a hard time with that when they were first together, and I think he still has trouble with it when she comes home smelling like her dad. Christ, are you going to come like this?" She told him she hoped so. "I'd very much like to have my cat mark you."

Everything stilled. She sat on him and watched his face. Mason was afraid that he'd upset her, and when she rolled off him, his cock wet with her juices, she stood up over him and put out her hand.

"Will he want to have sex with me? I'm not sure that's something I'd want." His cat snarled at him, and he calmed him by telling him that they were working on it. "I don't know what marking means really, except that he bites me, but if he tries to have sex with me, I might just kill you both."

Mason stayed where he was but took her outstretched hand. "He won't have sex with your human self. If you ever want to become a cat, then he will with your cougar. But he does want to taste your pussy. I think it's to get your scent; or he could just want to drink from you like I do."

"You mean eat me." Mason nodded and rubbed his head on her hand, and let his cat take him. He wasn't going to scare her, but his cat really wanted his part of their mate. "What do I do? And I'm serious about the sex part. I'm not going to do it."

Spread your legs just enough for him to get your scent. She moved back, not running but moving away from them. Before he could tell her not to run, she leaned against a tree and opened her legs. His cat moved toward her like he was stalking prey, and he had to caution him not to hurt her.

His cat was very aggressive, like all cats, but his was leader and his mate was denying him all she was. When he buried his nose between Emma's legs, Mason told him again to be careful. He shouldn't have worried. The moment his tongue touched her, Emma came, screaming, and curled her fingers into his fur.

"Again. Give me…I want more." His cat fucked her with his tongue, moving in and out of her sheath much like Mason had with his cock. She came twice more, her body dewy with her excursions.

When she begged him to stop, Mason watched her when the cat pulled back. She was hanging onto the branch above her and her body was lax with her release. But when his cat lunged forward again, Mason didn't have time to warn her of what he was going to do when he bit her. Emma screamed, this time in pain, and he felt his heart break.

It was over quickly. As soon as his cat let him go, Mason stood up and pulled her into his arms. The bite was deep, he knew that, and more than likely very painful. But when she cupped his cock in her hand, Mason looked down at her and asked her what she was doing.

"I want you to fuck me." Mason only stared at her and when she spoke again, his cock seemed to have a mind of its own and hardened incredibly more. "You owe me after that. And to feel you deep inside of me makes me as wet as you are hard. Please, Mason, just fuck me like you want to."

He turned her around and bent her at the waist. Entering her hard, he fucked her this way as she held onto the lower branch for support. Leaning over her, he told her what he was going to do and bit her again. Tearing into her skin would leave a scar, but he wanted the world to know that she was his. Sliding his fingers over her clit while he took her, he told her to come, to let go, and when she did, he filled her again and again, knowing that for as long as he lived, she was his.

Holding her upright when she told him she was hurting, Mason didn't speak. There was so much going on in his head right now, he wasn't even sure where to start. But when she pulled away, Mason looked at her body and realized just how rough he'd been on her. It was hard not to smile at how well she'd taken him on.

As he dressed, he watched her. She'd not said a word in the last ten minutes, and he was afraid that he'd hurt her. Not physically, no. Those wounds, the ones from his cat and himself, were healed up and she didn't seem to favor them, but something was wrong.

"I live in the city." Mason nodded, not sure what that had to do with anything. "I know you're a rancher. I'm not quitting my job just because you think you own me."

"I'm not sure how it is you think I own you, but why would I want you to quit your job?" Her shrug wasn't very informing. "Emma, look at me."

Her shirt came down over her body, and he watched her pull her shoes on. She'd not answered him or looked at him, and Mason felt his temper slide up. When she stood up and started for the house, he stopped her by jerking her around. Her fist connected with his mouth even as he started to talk.

"What the fuck are you doing?" She only stared at him until he wiped the blood away. "Are you always this violent when you're pissy?"

"I'm not pissy." He cocked a brow at her. "Okay, I'm a little pissy. But you grabbed me. I'm able to defend myself when I'm threatened."

"Do you feel threatened?" When she didn't answer him, Mason stepped closer to her and was glad that she didn't move away. "Do I threaten you? In any way?"

"No." She looked frustrated and he waited. There was something she wanted to say, and he knew that she had to tell him. "My brother. He's…he's hit me before. Recently. I took some defense classes so I'd…when those men attacked me, I thought that Dirk had sent them to rough me up because I wouldn't give him what he wanted."

"And what was that?" She didn't look at him and when she finally did, he could see her fear. It was tangible and strong. He pulled her into his arms and held her while asking her again what he'd wanted.

"He wanted me to tell him what Dad and Mom's will said. Dirk wanted to be sure that I wasn't getting more than him or, for that matter, I was getting a great deal less than him. I never told him, but he told me that he was the son and thought it best that he had all the ranch and money since I was working. I think…he said he had plans and a buyer already lined up. I doubt that is true. Dad said that he'd asked Dirk if he wanted a share of the ranch like I have, and he told him that he'd just wait until Dad died and have it all. I can't believe that he'd say that to him." Mason held her, trying to think what the fuck was wrong with the younger man. He had some serious god-like feelings going on there. "Mason, my dad changed his will about a month ago. Dirk is going to get an allowance and nothing more. Not any of the ranch, and none of the money that Dad has made over the years. He's getting three grand a month until he's thirty-nine. Then nothing. I'm afraid he's going to hurt me…really, I'm afraid he'll kill me when he finds out. Mom and Dad too."

"I'm going to tell you something. Please just listen to me before you get angry, okay?" She nodded. "Your dad has made a deal with me. I'm going to take over the running of the ranch a little at a time until you and I decide to get married. If you'll marry me, then we'll both have it. I'm not asking you to marry me because…well, I don't want you to think that's the only reason I want to do it."

"I'm not ready to get married. I might not ever be." He nodded, and he could feel she was scared about them. He was too if he was honest about it. "Mason, we don't love each other. I'm not even sure…we might hate each other when we're not having sex. That alone can't make a life together."

"I know that. It's why I wanted to talk to you today. Before…before the shower, I wanted you to come to me so that I could tell you everything your dad wants. But I got sidetracked, and you are just too sexy to resist." She snorted and he laughed. "You can distract me whenever you want like that, but we really need to sit down and talk to your dad and mom. It's getting bad out there with Dirk, and we have to have a plan. That way you can tell them how you feel."

"You want to marry me?" He nodded, but told her that he didn't love her, not yet anyway. "I want a love life like my parents have. They love each other and respect one another's feelings too. I don't think we're there yet."

"You're right, we're not. But I want you to keep an open mind on the fact that my kind, all shifters, fall in love only once. And you are my mate. I will care for you, keep you safe, but I'm not going to rule you." He crossed his arms over her back, holding her tightly to him. "I might know more than you on a few things, like protecting you against men like your brother, but you know a great deal more about nearly anything else that I don't. I will never treat you as any less than my one and only."

She didn't say anything for several minutes, but he could feel her relaxing against him. When she looked up, pulling slightly away, he looked down into her eyes and smiled at her. Mason had never been in love before, and despite what he'd just said to her, he was pretty sure that he was as close to falling over the edge as anyone could ever be. And he wasn't the least bit upset about it.

"He's going to hurt one or all of us, isn't he?" Mason nodded. He wasn't going to lie to her. And he never wanted to keep things from her. He knew that it could get one or both of them hurt. "And when he does, you're going to kill him."

"I will." She only stared at him before pulling away. Mason wasn't sure what she was going to do or even say about it, but when she turned back to him, he could see that she'd come to a decision.

"I wrote him off as never changing years ago. I don't think...not until recently have Mom and Dad, especially Dad, understood just how bad he has gotten. There are things...some things that I did for him that I'm not proud of. More than...I'll get you the file as soon as I get back to my house. But if you have to...if you have to take him out, I never want to know how. Just...just know that while he's the worst person I know, he's also my brother." He told her he understood. "Will you tell the rest of them as well? Your brothers?"

He told her he would and watched her walk back to the house after she told him she didn't want to know what they did either. Mason had things to finish here and when she was out of sight, he reached for his brother to keep an eye on her. When Jace said that he would, Mason closed the connection and got back to work. It was going to be a long day.

CHAPTER 7

Emma was just sitting there staring into space. Holly had tried twice now to get her attention but nothing was working. When Georgie came into the room, she told her what was going on with the other woman.

"Maybe she's mad at Mason. He's been acting really weird lately too. I heard him whistling yesterday morning." Holly had heard that too. It was as if he'd been turned into a pod person and this guy was always in a good mood. "I even tried to tell him we were having liver and onions for dinner, and all he did was smile and kiss me on the forehead. Perhaps they have some sort of bug."

"We're not sick." Holly grinned and looked at Emma when she finally spoke. "And for the record, I love liver and onions. But we're not sick. He told me...I guess if I didn't want to know, then I shouldn't have asked."

"Asked what?" They were in her house and Holly got up to get them all some cookies and tea. When they were younger, Emma would only eat chocolate chips, and Holly wondered if she'd broadened her taste buds since then. Holly was feeling much better. Whatever was in that brew that she'd been given to make her feel better, she was going to get the ingredients so she could have it around. "You want hot or cold tea?"

"Cold; and I asked him about my brother. He told me that if he hurt any of us, he'd kill him. Well, I asked him if he would and he said he would. I guessed really. I asked him and he answered me, so—"

"Emma." Her mouth snapped closed when she looked at Georgie. That was something else, Emma never babbled, but she was doing that a lot lately too. Georgie smiled at her and continued. "Now, take a deep breath and tell us what you're talking about. We understand that Mason is going to protect you, but why did you ask if you didn't want to know?"

"I did want to know. I do now still." She got up to pace, and Holly handed her a glass of iced tea. "I get this protection thing. I looked it up last night about cougars. I guess…you know, there is nothing on the Internet about them…shifters, I mean? Well, there is a little—lore they called it—but Christ, you'd think they changed into these monsters and made these god-awful messes when they did it."

"Yes, and we would like to keep it that way." Georgie asked Emma to have a seat and when she was seated, Georgie handed her the same book she'd been given when she'd been converted. "Guard this with your life. It's everything you might want to know or information you might need being mated to a shifter. When you've read it and get a grip on what is going on, then give it back please. I have other nephews that might need it."

Emma stared at the book as she spoke. "He told me that he wants to protect me, but that I'm smarter than him. And he said that while he didn't love me yet, he would fall in love with me much faster because of what he is." Emma looked up at them both. "What if he's wrong about me? What if...what if he really just wanted sex really badly and I was there and willing?"

"He is your mate. I'm sure that you're overwhelmed at the moment. It's a lot to take in, along with your brother and the mess he's causing. But trust me, honey, he's your mate and you're his." Georgie patted her hand as she continued. "Now, you're supposed to tell me what kind of meals you like to eat and what sort of house you're thinking of wanting."

"House?" Holly nodded when she looked at her. "I guess I never thought about it. I have an apartment in the city, and there's this house out on my parent's property that is mine. It was the first house that was built here. There was a shack at one time, but it was torn down when Grandmother built this house. Dad gave it to me when I went to college. Would you like to go out and see it?"

They were loading in the car a few minutes later. Holly listened to Emma as she told them that when she'd been sixteen her grandmother had passed away, and that the house had been handed down to Emma when her mother passed. Emma and her grandma had been very close.

"It nearly killed me when she died. But she was doing things she loved and that's what made her passing better. Can you imagine an eighty-year-old woman learning to ski? She got a cold, and then pneumonia. It was quick, I guess, but I miss her more every day." The car slowed to turn onto a drive that was lined with trees on both sides. "Dad has someone come out and clean it every week. I have no idea why. I think he's hoping that I'll move in and drive to work every day. I suppose I could...it's only about a forty-minute drive."

Holly's breath caught when she saw the house. It was, in a word, gorgeous. And it looked like something from the old southern movie about Georgia and the winning of the war. She could just see Rhett standing on the front porch waiting on his one true love. When she got out, she stared at the house like Georgie did...with her mouth hanging open.

The six tall pillars were a bright white. There were at least a dozen equally white rockers on the big porch, and the veranda on the second level had them as well, with a long roof that hung down over the steps leading up to the front door. The double front door made of what looked like oak was brilliant in the sunlight, with all the cut glass sparkling out over the porch and lawn. The brick was all dark, and the shutters that surrounded the windows were as white as the pillars as well.

Chimneys graced each end of the house, and there was a third one in the very back that stood as proudly as the trees up the drive. The windows, four on the bottom level and four on the top, were floor-to-ceiling, and Holly would bet that the entire house had windows like them all the way around it. When they went up the front steps, a younger man came out to greet them.

"Miss Emma, we didn't expect you today. Mr. McBride had us come out and have the house given a good overhaul. He thought you'd be bringing out your future husband soon." The man bowed to them both, and Holly had an uncontrollable urge to curtsy. The man just screamed old south. "I have some tea if you'd like. I can have you set up in the parlor. We're doing some work on the master suite. There was a problem with the roof, and we'll be working on it all week. If you want to go there, just let me know." Emma nodded as she led them into the house.

"Can you have some lunch made for us too? I'm going to show them around. Oh, and this is my future husband's Aunt Georgie, and his sister-in-law Holly Douglas. Guys, this is Randy Byrd. Randy and his family have been working this house since my great-great grandmother had it built back when big houses were the thing to do." He took their purses and told Emma that lunch would be ready when they were. He seemed to just blend into the house as he disappeared.

They started on the lower level. There was a dining room that would serve fifty people easily, and enough plates and things in the sideboard and cupboards to feed that many more. Silver had been laid out and someone was polishing it. Holly looked at the large D in the middle of the handle and laughed.

"I never even thought of that. My great grandmother had this with her first husband, who sadly died when she was very young. Her name then was Detroit. Believe it or not, his first name was Johnny. Grandmother used to tell me stories about him that would curl your hair, as she used to say." Emma picked up a framed picture that was lying on the table as well to be polished. "This is them. He was a handsome devil."

When she put the picture back, they moved to the next room. It was the parlor, where a large tea trolley was just being rolled in with a three-tier dessert tray, as well as a silver tea pot and the smallest tea cups she'd ever seen. Holly was used to elegant, but this was beyond what she'd ever been exposed to.

After having several cookies as well as the best tea she'd ever had, Emma led them around to the rest of the lower level. There was a man's study that held the desk of her great-great grandfather, a library that had more books on the four levels than Holly would bet most library's had, as well as a small sitting room and a music room that held not only a baby grand piano, but a harp and a set of drums.

"My grandmother tried everything. At one time there was not just the drums, but a steel guitar and a bass. She was very much the adventurous type." Georgie said that Emma must take after her a great deal, and she only waved her off. Holly thought the two women were a lot alike, and had really liked the woman when she and Emma would have tea with her at the family house.

It took them four hours to go over the house, it was that big. The bedrooms on the upper levels had been renovated recently, and Emma was telling them that there were at one time eight rooms up here, and now there were only four.

"They were the smallest rooms you'd ever want to use. I know that they were for guests, and Grandmother used to say that they were made uncomfortable so that no one wanted to overstay their welcome. Dad and I discussed it awhile back and had them enlarged and bathrooms put in each one. At one time, when the house was built, there wasn't a bathroom on this floor at all, but a privy out back. Grandmother had a modern bath put in on each floor when she lived here, as well as a powder room off the living room." Georgie asked her where the master bedroom was. "It's on the first level off the living room and down a great long hall. It's a huge room that has a master bed, something bigger than a king in it, a sitting room, as well as a ladies bath and a master bathroom. I have no idea why. There are closets too, one for each of the people who use it. But you can see it from here."

The view was beautiful out the back of the house, where she showed them the room under construction. There were several large tarps that were covering the roof, but even from here, Holly could see that the room was massive.

A large pool sat between the two wings that looked to be as big as the front of the house. They had been added after the house was built, Emma told them. On the opposite side and to the left of the large office for the man of the house was a room that looked like it was twice that of the big bedrooms they were in now. All in all, this was a house made for someone with a great deal of money and no thought to how much it would cost to heat or cool it. And what Holly had compared to what Emma had was a world of difference, she thought.

~~~

Landon moved through the store like a man on a mission. Just what the mission was, he had no idea. His investor had told him this was where he needed to sink some money, and by God, the man had been right for years, and he wasn't going to turn him away now. When Holly entered the store a few minutes later, he greeted her with a huge hug, completely forgetting that she was mated.

"I'm sure he's going to be mad at me. Jace is a good boy, but he's a mite possessive." Holly laughed and told him it would be fine. "You shop here too? Anthony sent me here as an investor. I'm not even sure what it is I'm looking for."

"I'm helping her out." He nodded, knowing now that he'd invest if he had to use his last dime. "She's mostly doing online selling finally, and it's going well I think. The shop is a sort of storage area for now. I just came by to see what she needed from me, if anything. Her daughter, Tessa, is really up on this too."

They were taken to a large room just off the back of the shop. The place was dingy and needed some much needed renovations to make the lighting better, as well as some of the stations that had been set up as a shipping department better flowing. Doris came around her sewing table and hugged Holly tightly, sobbing about how well the shop was doing.

"Every hour we have to check the orders coming in. It's like…I never dreamed it would be this big. I'm working so much now…I'm just able to keep it all up and running with Tessa's help." Holly told her she was glad to have helped.

"Maybe you should hire a couple more to help out. There is any number of women out of work, and this would be something that they'd like, I think." Landon picked up the doll that looked like it was made all by hand. "This is beautiful. You make this too?"

"Everything. And what I can't make, we find and repurpose." While she explained what that meant, he looked around. "And I'm not ready to hire someone just yet. I don't know how long this will keep up, and I don't want to disappoint someone who I hire."

Landon was hardly paying attention. His mind was working on all kinds of ways to expand and grow. When she laughed, he looked over at Holly, knowing that he'd missed something.

"She was telling you about the order she just got and you zoned out." He nodded and sat down. "Landon, I don't think whatever is going on in your head is going to thrill Doris. She's afraid enough."

"The two of you will love it." He started talking and the more he spoke, the more excited he got. "There's a warehouse that I have down the street. It's perfect for you. Lots of room. Storage space out the butt. There is a large open air store on the lower level that is ready to move into, after a bit of painting and some more shelves. There's even some older furniture on the upper levels you can use as display. I have a desk up there that I had stored so long ago that I can't even remember why I thought I needed it."

"I can't do that." Landon was nodding even as Doris was continuing. "I can barely afford this place, and it's cheap. I mean, we're making money but…. We live upstairs so we can save money. I just want to make enough to support me and my daughter. Taking that building would put me in a deeper hole than I am in now."

"I'm investing in your company, my dear." Landon stood up and walked around the room she was using. "You can hire some of the people who work at the nursing home. My wife goes there once a week to do crafts with them. Some of them are fantastic. Not on the level you are, but they can do the small stuff. They could come here daily, work out a little, then go back. Most of them would do it for little to nothing. Then there is the…"

Holly put her hand on his mouth, and he grinned around it. "You're making her insane. You know that, don't you? Just calm down and help her, not take over. What is your plan? I'm sure you have one."

"Yes I do. I want to invest, like I said, and help you to grow big enough that not only are you saving a lot of money, but you're investing in your future too." Doris did look scared, and when Tessa came back to ask about a piece, she left with her daughter and Landon looked at Holly. "I think I screwed up, didn't I?"

"Maybe, but I'll talk to her. The warehouse, where is it?" He told her. "I have two buildings right around there. I've been thinking of doing some renovating myself. I have a woman that wants to rent one to sell antiques in it. Then the other I was thinking of studio apartments. Rent them out to some of the urban up and coming that are working downtown. Did you know that since we've reopened the bank and the other shops that Rogers was in charge of, we've had an increase of ten percent of people moving in? Also five new store fronts, including this one."

He'd known that the town was coming from a near death sentence...something else that he knew that the Douglas men were a part of. The more he found out about them, the entire family, the more he was glad that Emma was going to be taken care of by Mason. Landon sat down and waited for Holly to do the same.

"I'm dying." She nodded. "Yeah, I thought you might know. Mason does as well. I think that's why he tolerates me so much when he wants more than anything to be alone. He's a good man."

"He's the best, I think. All of them are. But that's not why you're here making noises about investing, is it?" He nodded, then shook his head. "My dad said you went by to see him yesterday. That you were checking up on a few things. Anything I can help you with?"

"My son." Holly didn't say it, but he could see that she was aware of what Dirk had been up to. "I've cut him out. Of everything in my life. It was that or have him drag us down. The doctor told me I needed less stress, and that was hard with him...I'm at fault, I know that, but I really didn't realize what I'd done until recently."

"You had nothing to do with the type of person he is, Landon. There are just bad seeds sometimes. And you might have overindulged him, but you didn't create the monster that he's become." Landon didn't even correct her. Dirk was a monster. "I heard about the hotel."

"There was so much damage done to that single room that they've had to have that room closed permanently. I went by and saw it. It looked like he'd taken a hammer to some of the walls. Why? Why would he do that?" She said because he could. "That's no reason. And I never raised him to be like that. Like you said, we overindulged him, but he's just…just not right."

"Mason said that he tried to talk to him about what was going to happen. He said Dirk never got it. He kept talking how you were going to come around. He wanted to know where the rest of his money was, and that he was going to give you a list of things he'd need weekly." Landon nodded and handed her the paper that had been delivered to his offices that morning. Landon said nothing as she read it over. "I'm sorry, Landon. He's out of control."

"He is. I've talked it over with my business attorney. I didn't want to involve Emma in this unless it came to that, but he's done. I've not disowned him, but unless things change and soon, he's not getting a penny from me. And I've made sure that he knows why, too, when it comes to that." Landon felt his heart twist in his chest over what he'd had to do. "Mason is a good man, like I said, and he'll make sure that my wishes are carried out. He might not like being a ranch baron, but he'll be good at it."

"He will. Emma took us by her house today. You're getting it ready for them, aren't you?" Landon felt his face heat up as he nodded. "I think she'll bring Mason around to living there as well. I'm sure you know that he, like the rest of the Douglas men, aren't used to having money."

"Hell, honey, they didn't have a pot to piss in, and now look at them. And that husband of yours, Jace, that boy has come a long way too. And not a dime of the money he spends is spent on things that he shouldn't. Not only is he careful with every bit that he spends, but he's making real progress in making that ranch of his the model of all ranches. Mason is helping him with that too."

They both turned when Tessa and her mother came back in the room. Landon stood up and watched the two of them. He'd bet real money that the daughter was the real business sense in the family, and that Mom trusted her more than she did money in front of her. "Ladies, I think I owe you an apology. I'm a bit over excited when I see something that I like."

"You are an overbearing turd is what you are." Doris flushed and Landon laughed. "I'm sorry. I'm trying my best not to be terrified out of my bloomers, and my daughter said it's good to be scared. But I want everything you're going to help us with in writing. And I want the option of telling you to leave us alone if that's what it comes to."

"Deal." Landon put out his hand and Tessa took it with a grin. Doris only stared at it. "I promise you that I'm only going to help you out. It's what I do and enjoy doing. As for the warehouse, I'm just trying to keep it from being taken over by the homeless. Not that they don't need a place to stay, but I'm working on that too."

"You would be." Doris sat down. "Now. About these women you said that might be willing to come in and work for me. I need to know how to contact them. And I'm not going to hire them just because you say so. I've got to make money, and having bad stuff made isn't going to cut it."

Three hours later, over dinner with his new partners and his wife, Landon felt really good about what he was doing. He'd been wrong about Doris. She had a good head on her shoulders and she was the kind of person he liked…no nonsense, and straight up telling you when she didn't like something.

Landon and Katie left the little restaurant feeling pretty good about things. When they got to their car and he put his lovely bride inside, he fell to his knees. The pain, whatever it was, had taken him to the ground.

"Dad, what are you doing to me?" He looked up at Dirk and almost didn't recognize him. It had only been a few days, three he thought, and Dirk looked like he'd been out on the streets for months. "Give me my money and I'll forget this ever happened. And I want a key to the house. You changed the locks. That wasn't very smart of you."

Landon looked in the car when he heard his wife talking. He hoped she was calling the police, because when his head exploded in pain again, he knew that he was going to die. Dirk was screaming at him to give him what he wanted, and when Landon felt himself being flipped over, he saw the bat that his son had been hitting him with. Landon closed his eyes and knew there was no hope for his child after this. None at all.

CHAPTER 8

Mason was in the emergency room when Emma came in. His family was there as well, having been in town. Emma had been at the mall when he'd contacted her, and she had to wait on the police to go and get her. Mason hadn't wanted her driving as upset as she was.

"Where is he?" Mason told her that her dad was still in surgery. "My mom? Is she okay? Did he hurt her too?"

"No. She didn't get out of the car and called the police as soon as she saw what was happening. Then she called me. She told me to get you but not to let you drive. She's in the waiting room."

Emma turned, then came back to him. Mason held her while she sobbed on his chest, and then helped her sit down when her knees seemed to give out on her. Holding her on his lap, he told her what he knew and what they'd been able to find out.

"Dirk saw the car when he was roaming the streets, we guess. He was waiting on them with a bat. Lucky for your mom, your dad is a gentleman and put her in the car before he got in. Otherwise we're not sure what would have happened." He knew as surely as he was sitting there that Dirk would have hurt his mom as well. "He hit your dad several times, once in the back and twice in the head. He's got several broken ribs, as well as a broken left arm. They're not thinking there's any permanent brain damage right now, but they have gone in to relieve the pressure from the trauma. His leg, the right one, is hurt. The knee is pretty bad, but they think that's from him falling rather than being hit."

"Did the police catch Dirk?" He told her by the time the police had arrived, Dirk was gone, but he'd left the bat with his prints on it. "When they find him they'll arrest him and put him in jail for a long time. This is attempted homicide. Not to mention premeditated...he had a bat with him. It's not going to look good for him at all."

"I'm sorry, honey." She asked him why. "I should have warned your dad to be more careful. I figured that Dirk would do something like this, just not so...he could have killed him over money. How could he...why? I thought he'd be on me, but not your dad. I just keep thinking about what if your mom had been out there as well." She shivered in his arms before speaking again.

"Can you take me to see Mom? I think...I have to be with her." Mason stood up, but didn't put Emma down just yet. "Mason, I'm sorry you're being brought into this. It's not exactly a nice family that you're going to be a part of."

"The only person I really care about is you. I like your mom and dad a great deal, but it's you I worry about the most." She nodded. "Emma, he won't stop. You mom said that he kept telling your dad to give him what he wanted and things would go better for him. And he tried to rob him. He didn't get anything but the car keys. I had no idea that your dad didn't carry a wallet."

"No. It's in the car all the time if he's driving. Or Mom would have had it in her purse. He hates the way it makes him feel, he told me once. Like he was off balanced somehow." Mason had heard him saying something similar when he was on horseback. He liked his balance. "I'm ready now."

Mason took her to the waiting room, and Katie and Emma held each other while they sobbed. He had no idea what to do now, and stood there watching them as Jace came to stand beside him. He asked to speak to him privately. They moved down the hall until they found an empty room.

"I have a buddy on the force, and they have found Dirk's prints all over the car as well as the bat. And two mornings ago it looks like he might have caused a ruckus at one of the department stores on Jelly Street." Mason asked him what sort of ruckus. "He messed up one of the clerks when he tried to tell him that he had no credit there. Dirk apparently told him in no uncertain terms that he, Dirk McBride, was going to get some clothing and he was taking it now. He also told them to bill his dad. There was bloodshed…not like today, but enough that the young man is off for a few days. He beat him with a mannequin arm."

"How come we didn't hear about it until now?" Jace just shrugged. "They're trying to keep the family out of it now, aren't they? I guess I'd do the same if I was them."

"Pretty much. They know that Landon is trying his best to handle this, and they know how much pressure the man has been under lately. I'm thinking they're hoping that one of them will run into Dirk and shoot him dead for Landon." That sounded like a good plan to him as well. "Mason, I've been thinking, and I don't think you should have much to do with Dirk from now on."

"Why the hell not? The man is a menace and he's hurt one of our friends. How can you even ask me to step down?" Jace looked around, then back at him as his temper seemed to grab him by the throat and his cat snarled at him. When he was pushed against the wall, Jace was almost nose to nose with him. "You're fucking with the wrong guy, little brother."

"If you kill him or even take him down, what do you think that is going to do with your relationship with Emma? I know that she's telling you to help her with this. And you told me that Landon pretty much told you the same thing. But what will happen if you kill him?" Mason started to tell him it wouldn't come to that, but was cut off. "Yes, it will. Dirk is going to provoke you until you have no choice. But I will say this…if he touches Emma, then you can fucking do what you want to him. I'll even help you."

"So, I just let this thing with Landon go?" Jace told him to let the police handle it for now. "And what if they don't do shit? Then what? Leave him out there to hurt someone else? Like Holly?"

"No, that's not what I'm saying at all and you fucking know it. What I'm telling you is to try your best not to be the one that kills him. You might have to, but I'd try really hard not to if I were you." Mason nodded but didn't promise anything. "Mason, this guy, what the fuck is wrong with him? I mean, how the hell could he do this to his own family? To his own dad?"

"I don't know. I've been looking things up." The two of them made their way toward the waiting room as they spoke. "I thought he was a psychopath, but that's not what he is. Not completely anyway. He has the whole not being responsible for a thing going for him, and no remorse or shame for what he's done. Dirk has always been stubbornly contrary to what most people would think is right and proper. So there is that. But I don't…it's hard to say."

"Is he a sociopath?" Mason told him no on that as well. "But there is something wrong with him in the noodle, right? I mean, who treats their family that way and thinks it's all right?"

He told him he had no idea but that he was looking up as much as he could. Mason told Jace he was exhausted all the time lately. Not all of it had to do with Emma and that they couldn't seem to get enough of each other, but the simple fact that he was running two ranches as best he could and it wasn't easy.

"I know. I'm...we're used to doing this all on our own and it's...I had to finally ask for help. I thought that I could do it all too and, fuck, it was hard. But Palmer told me that he was waiting for me to figure it out on my own. Damned near killed myself for him trying to prove a point."

They were both still laughing as they made their way back to the waiting room. Mason was going to have to ask for help, and soon. It was that or have a heart attack trying to keep up with Emma and the ranch.

Emma was sitting with her mom and their aunt when they entered the little room. Palmer was there, as well as the rest of his brothers. The sheriff had shown up as well. Howard LeBlanc, who had started the week after the mill was finally closed up, was a nice guy and Mason really liked him. This guy was a man to fear if you were a fuck up, and one to trust if you needed him.

"I'd like a word with Mrs. McBride if you think she'll be all right." Mason wanted to shield the woman from any kind of questions right now, but Emma came over and told him she was ready. Mason went to the little room too, after it was established that he was the future son-in-law. Also, that he wasn't leaving. LeBlanc nodded once and told him to behave if he was staying.

"Mrs. McBride, can you tell me what you heard when your husband was hurt?" Mason started to tell him it was her son, but he was pretty sure that he knew that. "We're looking into all kinds of things that might have led up to what happened, and we're to understand that you and your husband had a falling out, sort of, with your oldest child."

"We've been having some problems with him for some time now, and Landon—that's my husband—and I talked it over and we decided that he needed to learn to stand on his own two feet. The boy has been…well, not draining us dry, but he's going to if we don't do something now. We had some help there with Mason and we turned him out." She looked up at LeBlanc. "Do you think this is our fault? That my son is doing this because of us?"

"No, ma'am, I don't. I think that your son is out of control, if you want to know the truth of it, and has to be taught a lesson. I've taken the liberty of going over a file that had his name on it before I got the call about your husband, and it's a small wonder he's not done something like this before." LeBlanc sat down now and pushed a file at Emma. "You're an attorney, right? You've been helping your brother on a few things that should have put him in jail."

"Now wait a fucking minute." Mason was cut off when Emma lifted her hand up. She looked at the sheriff and nodded.

"I've gotten him time served on two things that should have been serious jail time, and once…he murdered a man, and I was able to get that brought down to a lesser charge. He never served any jail time because…well, not to brag, but I'm that good. Or that stupid. Lately I'm not sure I did the right thing."

"It's family, and you can't help but be there for them even when you think it's not right. I know." LeBlanc took the file back and turned to something in the back. "This is from four years ago. Another murder he wasn't even slapped on the wrist for. The other sheriff gave him a pat on the back for killing someone that was, in his words, 'undesirable.' I'm still trying to figure out what that was supposed to mean. But the man is dead, and now I have another problem on my hands. Your son is on a path that is going to get him killed sooner rather than later, I'm afraid."

"He kept telling my husband what he was going to do. 'Give me the keys. I want my money back. You're going to let me come home now.' He was never loud until...until Landon wasn't conscious anymore. Then he was screaming at him." Katie shivered and looked at him. "I called the police when he hit Landon the first time. Then I called Mason here. He held me on the line the entire time, telling me not to get out of the car. He was sure that he would have killed me as well."

"I believe he was right. And in the future, I'd very much like for you to come and go off the ranch with someone like Mason or one your hands every time until we can resolve this. He's going to hurt you, of that I've no doubt." LeBlanc asked her again what had happened.

"We were coming out of the restaurant. I didn't see Dirk until his father went down. When I realized what was happening, I started to get out but then thought that I needed to call someone. Like I said, Mason told me to stay put. But Dirk was...I remember thinking the entire time he was hurting his father, it was as if he had no clue that he was hurting him. His face was as calm and as serene as if he were asking him for a cup of tea or something. But his voice. It was so hard and cold. I'd never heard him speak like that before." She looked at LeBlanc before she continued. "I'd very much like it if you were to find him soon. I'm not sure that he's not going to hurt someone else. Mason for sure. Dirk said a few times that Landon was going to stop taking orders from him, and that he wasn't marrying his sister. Dirk said that Emma would die if she married him. I wondered at the time if he was planning to kill her if she did."

"Did he take his money, any credit cards?" Katie told him her husband didn't carry a wallet, that she'd had it in her purse. "Did you know that your son had a gun, and that he planned on using it on one of you?"

"No. I know that he used to hate them. Once when the kids were smaller, Landon took them hunting. He said it was for them to learn how to live off the land. Emma loved it and got a deer, but Dirk had told us that night that if he ever had to kill something and then dress it for his supper, he'd just as soon kill a hunter than an animal." Mason shook his head at that. Katie started crying softly as she spoke again. "I only just remembered something else he said. He told Landon that if he even heard that Mason was in the will, that he'd kill him before his father was cold in the grave. Why does it matter to him who we have in our will or not?"

No one answered her and after a few more questions, LeBlanc left them. He said that he'd have someone outside the door to Landon's room, and that he was going to make sure that they did a few extra drive-bys at the house too.

Mason sat down when he left them. Katie took his hand in hers.

"I know that you're not married and all, but I'd very much like it if you moved in with us. I'd feel much better about it knowing that we had someone there that's a little above the normal police officer. I suppose that I should have talked this over with Emma, but I'm afraid of Dirk." She laughed bitterly. "Who would have ever thought I'd say those words about my own child?"

Emma held her mother while she cried, and Mason tried to think how this would work. When Emma touched his mind, he felt like he was in deep trouble when she told him that she'd feel better as well.

I don't trust that he shouldn't be able to get inside. And if he does, then he will hurt us. There is no doubt about it now. He told her that he agreed. *Mason, I know that you're afraid to hurt Dirk...that maybe I'll be pissed at you or something, but right now if he were here, I'd tear his fucking throat out.*

Mason said he would move in with them. But instead of going to the house where she'd grown up, they decided that they should move into the house that belonged to Emma. Katie wasn't even sure that Dirk was aware of the house, and they might be safer. Mason figured that a smaller house might be easier for him to protect.

Mason nearly fell over when they pulled up in front of the "little" house.

~~~

Dirk sat at the table and watched the news. Why they were making a big deal out of this was beyond him. His father was hurt, so what? It wasn't as if he couldn't afford the best care to get better. And had he just done what Dirk has asked him to do, then things would have been better for him. Dirk thought about the conversation he'd had with his dad just before he left to find something stronger to hit him with.

"I don't know why you're doing this to yourself. I just want what is mine. What is your problem with that?" He'd hit him in the head with the bat he'd brought with him.

"Dad, don't ignore me. I just want you to hand over your wallet with the cards in it, and I'll go back to the house and wait for you to bring me some cash. Everything will be just fine then."

The bat had broken when he'd hit him again. It might not have had his father not parked so close to the curb. His father was being very inconvenient, and the sooner he just gave him what he wanted, things would go back to normal. Well, as normal as they could be now that he no longer trusted them.

The timer dinged on the microwave and he got up to see to his meal. It was his third such meal in the last twenty minutes, and he was getting pissed about how very little there was in the container. There was no point in going out to talk to the woman who was in the house before him. Dirk had discovered that she had died at some point, and now he had no one to fix this for him.

The house he was in wasn't his own. Not only was it much smaller than his home, but this one had no servants. But he needed a place to stay and there was an open garage door that led into the house. The woman that was in the kitchen when he came in had startled him or he wouldn't have had to hit her to quiet her. His head was pounding, and she should have known better than to do that.

The meal was done, but it looked odd. He read the name on the front again, and this didn't look like any chicken Alfredo that he'd ever eaten. Dirk thought about calling the manufacturer again but wasn't willing to wait on hold again. The last time it had been five minutes, and he had better things to do with his time. And no matter how much he looked, there wasn't a special number for the wealthy to use written anywhere on the box, nor was there a number to press for it on their tree. He ate most of this one and tossed it away like he had the other meals that weren't up to par.

Dirk wasn't happy with the way things were going. Not having any way to get around other than walking was making him sore and cranky. Then there was the fact that he couldn't party either. He'd had to roll a man last night for enough drugs to get him just a little high, and then had gone back and killed him for it being inferior stuff. His parents and his sister had a lot to answer for when they got him back home. Not to mention the messes that were piling up because of the way he'd been treated. Dirk looked up at the television again when he heard his name. Finding the remote, he turned it up.

"...last night, leaving one man dead and two more injured. Dirk McBride is considered to be armed and dangerous at this hour, and the police would like for you to call the number on the screen rather than approach him. To repeat, Dirk McBride is wanted for questioning in the death of Pavel Dillinger, as well as the robbery of the *Gas and Go* on Fourth Street that left two men fighting for their lives. We'll keep you updated on more information as we get it."

Dirk wrote the number down. There were some things that they were missing, and he wanted to call them and straighten them out. First of all, he didn't kill Dillinger, whoever that might be. And if it was the drug guy he'd rolled then went back to kill, it wasn't his fault. If you were going to try and sell him crappy shit, then you had to pay the consequences. As for the *Gas and Go*? He'd only beat them up because they refused to give him the combination to the safe. He no more believed the sign that said it was on a timer than he did the man begging him for his life because he was getting married. Who the fuck cared if you were going to shackle yourself to a woman or whatever? Dirk McBride came first in all things.

"Fucking bastards." He got up to pace. "I'm not the bad guy in this. It's Mason Douglas. He thought he'd be such a big man and have my parents who love me teach me a lesson. I don't even know what the lesson is, but I'm out of my home, no money to spend, and my best shirt is ruined because my dad is a stubborn old fool."

The news played on in the background and he paused when he heard his nemesis' name. "Mason Douglas and his brother Jace are still looking for donations to help with the family that was burned out of their home last week. Linens as well as simple cleaning supplies are needed, as well as beds. The family lost everything in the fire, including their little puppy, Bigalow." The newscaster turned to the man sitting next to her as she continued. "I heard just before coming on air this evening that someone donated a puppy to the two little girls. That was the sweetest thing, don't you think?"

Dirk picked up the chair and threw it at the television. There were people like him out of a place to live, and no one gave a shit about him. Who the fuck cared about a family that didn't have the sense to put out a fire when it started, compared to him and his losses?

As he made his way through the house, destroying what he could lift, he decided that he was going to take matters into his own hands and go and take care of the problem. And the problem was Mason. The man had caused him enough trouble, and it was time for him to be put back in his place...his sister too if she put up any kind of fuss. Dirk was the son of Landon and Katie McBride, and he was going to make them all sit up and take better care to remember that.

It took him three hours of searching the house for money before he found any. There was a purse in the kitchen when he'd arrived, but it was empty of even a wallet. Going from room to room looking for anything had made him even madder, and by the time he'd found the woman's stash, he nearly screamed in frustration when he realized how little she had for him. Four hundred dollars would barely pay for him a nice pair of pants and a shirt, much less get him out to his parents' house.

The car in the garage taunted him. Dirk have never learned how to drive a clutch, and considered it way beneath him to do so. Besides, there had always been a ride for him when he wasn't able to drive himself. The limo had been his to use whenever he wished, up until about a year ago when his dad had forbade him to take his friends in it. Then there was the woman that had been found in the trunk that had really pissed his father off.

"Big deal." His dad had told him it had cost a great deal of money to compensate the family for what he and his friends had done to her, and Dirk had argued it was nothing compared to what they'd done to the other woman. Dirk had been slapped for that, and he had never forgiven his father for that either. It wasn't like they'd killed them.

"You raped those women. Drugged them and raped them. What the hell were you thinking? or were you?" It had been a trick question, Dirk had known it, but he'd been too hung over and stoned to think. "Dirk? Answer me."

"Just fucking pay them off and let me get some sleep. Why the fuck do you care what I do so long as I'm happy?" His dad had walked away then and Dirk laughed. "You might want to keep the checkbook open, Dad. I'm betting you get a few more calls about last night too."

He supposed his dad had paid them off because he never heard another thing about it. His life had been perfect before Mason. He'd had what he wanted when he wanted it and how he needed it. Now it was all going in the wrong direction, and he wasn't going to stand for it any longer.

CHAPTER 9

Emma wasn't sure what was going on in Mason's mind, but she could tell that it was either pissed or overwhelmed. She tried her best to see this through his eyes, and thought it was a great deal of both. This was a house made for someone who had grown up this way, not someone who was just getting into it.

"Would you like to see our room?" He looked ready to bolt, and she put her hand over his heart. "Mason, this is our house, but if you don't like it we can sell it and move anywhere you think is better."

"This has been in your family for a while now, hasn't it?" She nodded and told him it didn't matter. "I don't want you to have to sell it, but...it's a big adjustment for me. I mean, a fucking huge adjustment."

"I know." One of the servants came into the living room where they were and told them that there was a phone call for Master Mason. Before he went with Sally, Mason leaned down to her ear.

"Can you please have them stop calling me Master Mason? I feel like I should be looking for another person every time someone does that to me." She giggled and he smiled at her. "I think I could get used to this, but it might take me a while. I expected…well, smaller. And a good deal less people in it to run it."

She was still laughing when he left her with a quick kiss. Her mom came into the room just as she was ready to ask one of the girls who were helping out try and get the televisions that had been delivered today hung up. Emma was scared when she looked at the girl who approached her.

"There's a man at the door. He told me to tell you that he cannot come in until you invite him." Emma moved toward her and stopped when the girl, Vicki she thought her name was, continued. "I know that you're aware of what we are now, so I wanted to let you know that this man is a vampire. He says he's a friend of your father's."

"Go and tell Mason that I need him. Also, there's a man in the back of the house, his name is Randy. Go and get him now." As she came out of the living room to the hall, not only was Mason there but Zach as well. The man at the door only stood there and smiled at them.

"My name is Monroe Hobbs. I've been a friend of your dad, Landon, for a good long time. Your mother knows me, though I don't know if she's aware that I'm not human." He looked at Mason and then at her again. "Your mate. A good man. Mason and his family have also been in my sights for some time now."

"Sights how?" Zach asked a very good question and Emma thought she'd like to know as well. "I know that your kind thinks our blood is better than human blood, but if you think we're letting you in so you can slaughter us, then you have to think again. You're not coming in."

"Hello, Monroe." He bowed low when her mom came into the room. "You got my message then?"

"I did. I've come to see if I could offer some help." Emma watched her mom go to the door to let him in. "I'm sorry, my lady, but the owner of this house must let me in. Or I'll just have to stay here and talk to them."

Her mom looked at her, then at Mason. "He's not human, I'm sure you're aware of that. I wasn't until a few weeks ago when Landon told me. He said that if he was ever on his death bed and not from the cancer, to make sure that I let Monroe know. Then he told me that he could protect me better than anyone. He told me this before you came into our lives."

Emma went to the door and Monroe stopped her from opening it. "He's your mate, my lady, and he will have to let me in. I'm aware that you are newly mated, but he is a master of his leap and he will need to welcome me."

Mason stood there without moving. She wanted to tell him if Monroe could help her dad, then he had better let the man in. But he crossed his arms over his chest and stared at him before speaking.

"What do you mean about us?" Monroe laughed and Mason took a step toward him. "I'm not fucking around here. My friend and future father-in-law is hurt, and if you want to help us, then answer the damned question."

"All right. There was a time when I owned the land on which you are living. Your parents—I am sorry for their deaths—came to me when I was ill and gave me something that few would give a vampire. I gave them the land in exchange for them keeping my...home...safe. After their deaths, I went to your aunt, a lovely woman, and told her of the deal. She, of course, knew about it and has honored me since." Monroe seemed to think something was funny and grinned hugely. "You're a great deal like your father, by the way. He was very stubborn as well until he realized that I had no intentions of harming his family. I will not harm yours either, Mason. You can trust me on that."

"My aunt said to ask you the date. I'm not sure what she means, but she said that only you would know, as you were there." Monroe nodded and gave him the date. "That's my birthdate."

"It is. And you should know that helping your mother bring you into the world was the greatest pleasure I've had in all my life. Your father was very…grateful that I was there to assist."

"She was dying." Monroe nodded as he turned to Emma. "You saved her life, and that's what made his dad trust you."

"You, my dear, are a great deal like your father as well. He was never one to sit idly by while things were going on around him. I should like to help him if you'd allow it." Mason told him he could enter, and Monroe came into the house. "Now. I'm to understand that he is grave? That they do not…shall we go?"

Monroe told them that he would meet them there. Her mom was standing in the hallway when she came down the stairs again. She looked…Emma thought she looked lost. Touching her fingers to her arm, her mom turned and looked at her.

"Your father…he was going to die. I just couldn't…I don't want to live without him, Emma. Not after all this time." Emma felt her heart twist in her chest and her mom cried. "He's my world, after you children. He can be contrary as all get out when he wants, but he's mine and I just…calling in Monroe was something that I promised your dad I would do. He thought…for years he's thought that Dirk was going to hurt us, but I…never in all my life would I have thought it was true. My son is a monster."

Emma couldn't even disagree with her. She'd seen the files that Mason had. And she'd been in the court room with her brother when he'd been arrested a few times. He was right, the McBride name had saved him and the money had gone a long way to buying things off. It wasn't until recently that she figured out that her brother wasn't sane. There was something very wrong with him.

They rode over in Zach's car. It was a little tight, but Mason had said that taking the limo to the hospital would just announce to Dirk where they were. So Zach had driven them. Emma laughed every time she looked at the way Mason had been stuffed in the front seat, and how he kept grumbling about a bigger ride.

"Hey, it's paid for, and I don't have to pay much in the way of insurance anymore." Zach winked at her in the mirror and smiled. "It's big enough for me and a girl should we have a need to get friendly."

Emma burst out laughing when her mom hit Zach in the back of the head. She wasn't sure if he'd forgotten she was back there or he was so used to being with his brothers that it never occurred to him to be a little discreet when talking about his sex-capades. If his red face was any indication, he'd forgotten her.

"Young man, I'm sure that whoever this young woman is would not appreciate you bantering her about as if she meant so little to you." He told her she was right. "Good. Now, you should go and buy her some flowers if all you did was have your…friendly taken care of."

Emma was still laughing at Zach when they entered the parking garage. Monroe was there waiting for them. To say she was scared would have been an understatement. But she was also aware that this man might be her father's only hope. She wondered what he was going to do, and decided that she didn't really want to know. So long as Dad was all right, then whatever it was, she was okay with it.

~~~

Mason wanted to tell the vampire to back off, but Aunt Georgie said that he was a good man and true to his word. It didn't make him feel much better, but it did help. As they entered the private room that Landon was in, Mason had to hold onto the bed when he looked at his friend.

His head was wrapped in gauze, but it was blood stained. His face was covered in not just the oxygen mask that was helping him breath, but a tube in his mouth that looked as if it too had blood in it. But what you could see of his face made Mason realize how old Landon was and how he'd suffered. Bruises and the dark thread of the stitches that they'd used to put him back together were a startling contrast to his pale skin.

His arm was tied to a board to hold the two IV's that were keeping the pain meds flowing. Landon's other arm was wrapped in a cast, as was his leg. It was lifted high off the bed in what could only be described as a crane and winch, but it was the monitors that had him standing back.

Several were beeping loudly. There was one that showed his heart beating, and on occasion it would show his blood pressure. Mason knew very little about such things, but he thought that a rate of sixty over thirty-five was bad, and his heart was only beating at twenty-two a minute. The nurse came in just as Monroe was moving to the bed. It took Monroe only a second to move her out of the room.

Before Monroe did anything, he looked at Katie. "He's close to dying, love. Soon, as a matter of fact. What I can do for him...I might be too late."

"Do what you can." He nodded and looked at Mason again. There was a question there, and Mason was sure he was asking him permission to do this. Also, Mason thought he was telling him that this might end worse than they all thought. When he nodded, Monroe nodded back and turned to the bed. As soon as he tore into his own wrist, Katie staggered. Zach caught her just as she would have fallen and sat her in the chair. Mason held onto Emma, as she too seemed a little wobbly on her feet.

It was over in a matter of minutes. There wasn't any improvement in Landon's health so far as Mason could see on the monitors, but Monroe sat down on the other chair and looked at him. He looked drained, and Mason felt sorry for him.

"You've not fed. You came right here." He nodded and told him he'd be fine. "You won't be and you know it. Why would you do something as irresponsible as that?"

"I told you that he was my friend." Mason nodded. "You would do the same should he ask you and you know it. I came as soon as I got the message."

"You're going to need to feed." Monroe asked him if he was volunteering and Mason told him he was. "Like you said, he's my friend as well, and as you have helped him, I would be honored should you allow me to help you."

"I cannot do that, young Mason. Should you wish to sever our relationship at any time, it cannot ever happen. I will know you as no one else would. We would forever be bonded." Mason moved toward the man, holding onto Emma's hand as he did so. When he let her go, it was to take off his jacket and bare his arm to him. Monroe stood up and pulled his arm to him to read the tat that Mason seldom thought about anymore.

"You're marked. I had no idea that you could hold ink once you shifted." Mason nodded and told him that all of his brothers had a tattoo, and they had no idea why they remained. "You're very special then. And this, what does it mean to you?"

He was talking about the tattoo. Mason looked at it and read aloud the words that he'd put there. "'Love is composed of a single soul inhabiting two bodies.' Aristotle. My mother used to tell me this all the time. That someday I'd meet my other half, and she'd help me conquer my other self. I had no idea what she meant until I met Emma."

"You love her." Mason nodded, only just realizing it himself. "Good, then you can understand why I will take your blood so freely offered. It is given with love, and the understanding that you care deeply and love hard for the same man and his family that I do."

"I do." Monroe took his wrist to his mouth and licked his pulse before biting him. There was no pain in it, and Mason had expected at least some. When he was finished, Monroe staggered back much like Katie had. Mason caught him before he fell and helped him to the chair.

"You're stronger than I thought, young cougar." Mason had no idea what that meant but nodded. "When you have children, I will come to you then. I should like to see them and to see if they carry the same strength as their father. I think they'll carry more of you than even I can imagine."

Before he could ask him what the hell he was talking about, the monitors behind him started to scream at them. The heart machine told that Landon's heart had stopped and was begging for someone to come and fix him. His blood pressure had dropped as well until it was a straight line. Katie started sobbing, holding onto Zach as she did. Mason felt his own tears fall down his checks as he held onto Emma, watching the man he'd come to love and respect die.

As nurses and doctors started to come into the room, the family was shoved back out of the way. The medical team worked for many long moments to bring Landon back, but to no avail. Emma was crying harder now, and Mason glanced over at Monroe. The man had not moved but stared at Landon intently.

Then the most extraordinary thing happened; Landon sat up.

The doctor that had the paddles in his hands fell backwards. He hit the floor hard, but didn't move to stand again. The nurse that had been holding a bag over Landon's face just stood there holding it out as if she were waiting for him to lie back down and be gone again. None of them moved, not the staff or the others in the room, until Landon spoke.

"By damn, I feel good." He looked around the room, then back at his wife. "Katie love, what's the matter? Did I make you mad at me again?"

Katie cried harder as she made her way to Landon. He held her to him as the staff, all of them silent still, moved around picking up fallen items that had come off the cart, as well as doing checks on the man who had been dead for too long to ignore. The doctor was helped up, and then he stood staring at Landon for several minutes before he just walked out. Another five minutes went by before the rest of the staff left them as well.

"You were gone and I thought I'd lost you for good." Landon had no idea what had happened if the look on his face was any indication, but he held his wife as she cried. "I don't want you to die without me. Promise me, Landan

McBride, or I will file for divorce right this minute and leave you to it."

"I promise. I'll…whatever you said." Landon looked over at Mason, then at Monroe. "You did this? I remember…Dirk hitting me, then waking up here. You helped me?"

"I did, with the help of Mason here." Mason started to tell him he'd done nothing, but Monroe continued, "He gave me what I needed to help you, Landon. Should he have been a selfish bastard like you are prone to be, I might have had to resort to going elsewhere for my dinner."

"You know as well as I do that you said you can't take my blood, you leech. And why is his so much better than mine would have been?" Landon wasn't mad but smiling. "I kid you not, I've never felt this good in a long time. I feel ten years younger."

"As you will for some time now. And you should know that the reason that I could not take your blood is no longer a problem. Had you asked, I could have healed you long ago." Landon stilled and Monroe nodded. "You are now as healthy as the young cougar is. You will remain so too, so long as you live."

"The cancer? It's gone?" Landon spoke so softly that Mason was sure that no one but him and Monroe could hear him. But Katie sat up and looked at Monroe as well, their need for the right answer clear in their faces.

"It is gone." Monroe backed away from the bed when it looked as if he were going to get a hug. But Emma caught him to her and hugged him tightly. Even his cat was all right with the contact, as he loved the old man as well. "You are as bad as a cat, my dear, and smell like one as well."

"Good." He let her kiss him on the cheek and then he turned to Mason. He'd forgotten that a link would be shared between them, and was surprised when Monroe spoke to him through it.

You and I, we must talk. This young son of theirs, he will not stop and you must know that. Mason told him he didn't think so either. *I will…watch over him, but not touch. I cannot for reasons I'm sure that you understand.*

You've given Landon your blood. Monroe told him that was part of it. *I've been warned not to kill him either. Jace, my brother, is afraid that it will cause bad feelings between me and the McBrides.*

He is more than likely correct. They won't mean to, but it will be there as a reminder all the time. I will keep an eye on him and keep you informed should he come to you and yours. Also, if he gets into any more trouble. I believe the man is on his way to becoming something of a problem to a great many people soon. Again, Mason agreed. *This bond between us, I should like to tell you that it is like any other I have with people, but you're different. Stronger than I thought, as I said, but you are not just a leader of your kind, but of all. You should run for office, young cougar. You will do much to keep this town back on the path to becoming viable again.*

I'm just a rancher that's trying to mete a living out of raising cows to produce milk. Monroe laughed and then looked at the people in the room. *You have done us all a great service. I will be indebted to you for a long time, if not forever.*

Nay, it is I who owes you. What you have allowed me to do is something that…he was dying long before his son hurt him, you are aware of that? Mason told him he was. *He will live for a great many more years now. His mate as well. You have…the children you will have with the young woman, they will make everything that happens soon so much easier to take.*

You know what's going to happen? Monroe told him only that the young man was going to meet with a bad end. *Will…this family, will any more of them be hurt by him?*

Not your family, no, but others will. Mason wanted to ask him who and how, but Monroe only shook his head. *I cannot tell you that should I even want to. You know as well as I do that he is in for a bloody end, and it will be the only way that there can be peace here. Dirk is…you've guessed that he is sick in the mind, but it has nothing to do with this family but of the way he was born. Having you here will keep anyone from dying, but some will get hurt. Be careful, my young friend, and I will be ever so grateful for it.*

I'll give it my best.

Monroe said his goodbyes and left them. Mason wanted to talk to him more about Dirk, but Landon was feeling so well that it was hard not to stay and talk to him.

A nurse came in with a glazed look on her face and removed all the plaster from Landon. When spoken to, she looked so confused that everyone just let her do what it was she was doing. When the last of the equipment was taken out of the room, Mason sat down and held Emma on his lap while she talked to her dad and mom.

The doctor returned some time later, and Mason knew that his mind had been altered slightly. He acted like Landon had only been in for a routine exam and had passed with flying colors. The only thing he cautioned him on was his diet.

"You'll need to eat better. More grain and vegetables. Also, I would like for you to take some time off. Maybe take a long trip with your wife and see the world from a ship. It will do you both a world of good." Landon said he was a rancher and raised beef, and the doctor nodded. "When you're having a steak, have a salad too. And not so much sour cream on your potatoes either."

When he left, Landon started bitching about men and their rules, and Mason just knew that in a few weeks, maybe sooner, Landon would be telling him how Katie was trying to kill him with food he hated. And Mason could not wait.

CHAPTER 10

Emma felt her body seem to come alive. Screaming as she came, she sat up and was shoved back on the bed when Mason continued to eat her. He had both her legs up over his shoulders as he devoured her. Emma knew that she was close again and held him to her as she felt herself coming again.

Christ, you taste delicious. I think I could feast on you like this every day and never get enough of you. She nodded to him, cupped her breasts, and tugged on her nipples. *That's it, baby, make them beg for me to suck them.*

When she came again, her body nearly bowing up off the bed, she watched as he moved back. Suddenly she was in bed with his cat and he dove at her pussy like he was starved. Even coming hard like she did before, she still came quickly when his tongue fucked her with long, sure strokes.

His tongue was so much different than Mason's. Not just in texture, but also in length and width. When he entered her, his tongue would touch in her ways that made her breath catch and her body scream for another release. When he curled his talented tongue around her clit and purred, Emma came again and again before she begged Mason to take her.

"You're beautiful when you come." Emma reached for Mason when he was leaning up on his knees. "And my cat loves the way you give him what he wants. You should see your face when he's feasting on you."

"He's good at it." Mason fisted his cock as she sat up and watched him. "I want you to fuck me now. Could you please? I want to feel your cock inside of me in the worst kind of way."

"I'd very much like to fuck you, but first I'd like for you to suck my cock." She moved on the bed while he leaned back on the headboard. He looked so good laying there that she stood up and looked at him while he continued to stroke his cock. "You like this, don't you? Me playing with my hard cock for you."

"Yes. I'd love to see you come like this. See it squirt out of your tip and come all over me." He moaned and she moved between his thighs. "Do it, Mason, come for me like this and make me come."

She slid her fingers down her body and into her pussy as he moved his hand up and down his cock. Precum gathered on the tip and she put her free hand there and gathered it before taking it to her pussy. His hand moved faster when she did that.

Leaning to him, she rolled her tongue around his crown before playing with the small slit. When she started to lift her head, he pushed her back to his cock.

"Don't leave me like this. Let me come down your throat, then I will fuck you hard." She moaned when he cupped her breast and squeezed hard. "Christ. Turn around, baby. I need to have all of you."

Not sure what he wanted, she moved when he pushed her into the direction he wanted. Lying with his cock right at her mouth, she was startled when he pulled her pussy up over his mouth and began to eat her. Taking his cock into her mouth, she nearly came when he bit down on her clit and started to fuck her mouth hard.

Emma loved the taste of him as he slid past her throat. Each time she swallowed him, taking him past the tight muscles in her throat, he would fuck her harder. And when he cried out, she felt his entire body stiffen just before he flooded her mouth with his cum. She was so intent on having him come that she'd forgotten about her own pleasure. When he pinched her clit again, she came apart crying out his name even as he came on her face and breasts. She was weak with her climaxes and thought that Mason might be as well.

She was flipped over so quickly that her breath caught. He was inside of her in seconds, his cock feeling thicker than before, longer too. When she wrapped her legs around his hips, he pounded her, giving her everything he had, and she found herself wanting more. Mason positioned her legs on his shoulders and lifted her ass up to him. She knew a whole new kind of pleasure when he leaned over her and suckled at her breast hard. Emma was bent in a way that gave her little room to move, but Christ, the pleasure was nearly too much.

Each time his cock touched her spot, she thought it was going to be the one, the climax that was going to kill her. But the harder he took her, the faster he fucked her, she knew that when she did come it was going to be the best ever. As soon as he bit down on her nipple, the pain of it bringing her over the edge, she pulled him down to her mouth and sank her teeth into his shoulder and tasted blood.

Coming harder now, she sucked at his blood. Every time it filled her mouth, she would swallow and come again and again. Mason raised his head from her body and threw back his head, and she felt him come, felt the cum splash inside of her as he filled her. When he growled, his cat moving along his skin like he wanted free as well, she knew that when he bit her this time it was going to be painful. And when he sank his teeth into her throat and growled, Emma lost her fight with consciousness and let the darkness take her.

When she woke, she was alone in the bed. Sitting up, she was sore and moaned when the pain in her body made her aware of what they'd been doing. Mason was sitting in the chair across from her and she stood up to go to him. When he said nothing, she straddled his lap and held him to her breast.

"I have to remember that you're only human." The soft breaths of his words made her nipples hard, and she moaned when he licked the hard tip. "You keep this up and I'm going to think that you're not finished with me."

"I want to ride you." He lifted her up, and she held onto his shoulders while he held his cock for her. Lowering her body over his, she could see how much he was enjoying this and slowed down to give him more. When she was seated as far as she could go, he cupped her ass and brought her to him over and over while she rolled her hips. "I love you fucking me. I could do this every day."

"I think I can help you with that." She moaned when he took her nipple into his mouth and nibbled. "I need to tell you something. It's really important."

She didn't want to hear anything right now but him calling out her name when he came. As she continued to move, he stopped her by pulling her body flush with his. His hand on her back and the other on her hip had her looking at him. Emma could see that whatever was bothering him was indeed important.

"If this is about Dirk, I really can't handle it right now." He shook his head. "Are you leaving me? If you are then...I don't want to hear that right now either. I've fallen in love with you, Mason, and right now if you tell me that you're going to—"

His mouth crushed over hers. It was hungry and powerful. It felt like he was giving her something to remember him by. One last kiss to make the leaving easier. Emma wrapped her arms around him and cried when he lifted his head.

"I wanted to tell you that I love you." She looked at him, tears still streaming down her face. "I think...no, that's not right...I *have* loved you from the moment you opened your eyes and looked at me. The second you stood up to me and told me off. I can't lose you. And I will never leave you." He held her then as she sobbed. Feeling stupid and a little on the vulnerable side, she looked up at him when he said her name.

"It's not much." She frowned, thinking she'd missed something. "I have a ring for you if you let me stand up and get it for you. I never thought...I should have with you, but I never thought you'd like sex as much as I do."

"You're very good." When he stood up, she felt his cock stretch. "Mason, let's get the ring later. Right now I want to finish what we've started."

Her back was pressed against the wall, and she moaned when he took her mouth again. Mason took her hard, and when he nuzzled into her throat she knew that he was going to bite her again. Tilting her head so that he could do what he wanted, she cried out her release when he bit her deeply, then came again as she felt his teeth tear into her tender skin.

Exhaustion took her then. As she closed her eyes, she heard Mason chuckle but didn't have the strength to even lift her hand to flip him off. This was his fault, he'd done this to her, and it was in her mind to tell him he could do this to her all the time when she just let sleep claim her.

~~~

Mason couldn't even get upset over the fact that his brothers weren't in a good mood too. Georgie told him that they'd been up late working to bring a calf into the world, and it had been a hard birth. Mason had already checked, and both mother and calf were doing well. Darin showed up about an hour after he got to work, and the rest of them staggered in a few minutes later.

"I've been meaning to ask you something." Darin was just hooking up the last of the cows to the milker when he spoke. "We need a breeder. Do you think that Landon would lend us a bull? Otherwise, we're going to have to go and get one off another ranch, and that didn't work out so well the last time. We could pay him going rate."

It hadn't. The owner of the bull had claimed that they'd overworked his prize bull. How the hell that was supposed to figure into it was beyond them. He claimed that he was going to sue for damages as well as future work that the bull could no longer preform. It was fucking; how the hell had they messed him up doing that?

But Palmer had done a little investigating and so had Holly, and they had found out that not only had he tried this bullshit before, but had been making a pretty good living at it. Needless to say, it was an open and shut case, and they were all the smarter for it.

"I'll ask him when I see him." They both turned when someone pounded on the door to the milking room. "Well, now you can ask him. I'm going to go and steal a few minutes with my mate."

Landon came into the room with them, and Mason took Emma with him to the office. He'd no more gotten her pressed against the wall to kiss her when the door to the office was being knocked on, and telling them to go away only generated laughter from the other side. Opening the door, he saw that Landon and Darin were there, as well as the police. Mason must have missed them.

"Hello, son." Mason flushed when Landon laughed again. "I'd hoped we catch you before it was too late. You do have a powerful need for my girl."

"I'm in love with her." Landon laughed harder. "And as soon as I can arrange it, I'm going to see about marrying her. Soon."

"Good for you guys. But that's about as obvious as the nose on your face." The police officer took his hand as he continued. "I'm really happy for you. But we've got…well, I've got a problem and I was hoping you'd be able to help me out with it. Landon said that you're running for office next term."

Before he could figure out what the hell he was talking about, both Darin and Emma were congratulating him. This was the first he'd heard about it, and he was having a hard time telling the people here that he had no desire to run.

"I'm just a rancher. I have…I don't know where they got this notion, but I don't want to run for anything, much less a public office." The cop, Officer Young, looked so disappointed that Mason wanted to tell him he was sorry.

He'd never said he'd run, and the next time he saw the fucking vamp he was going to murder him. He'd done this, he was sure of it. "Maybe we can help you with your problem, however."

"We need a mayor." Mason backed away, as if just saying it to him meant that he was going to take the job. "And soon. Without someone in office to give us the okay on some of the budget items, or even the hiring of some more officers, we're going to continue to have a hard time keeping up with the little crime we have here."

"I don't...I have no idea what that would even require." Emma took his hand and he had a thought. "My wife. She'd be really good at it. And she has a law degree that would keep your asses out of shit if you tried something like Rogers did."

"I can help you out in the meantime, but I have a job." Mason was so relieved that someone was going to do this that he nearly missed the look in Emma's eye. She was upset with him and he had no idea why. "I'll just have to make a few phone calls, but I think I can work as an intern until you get one to work full time."

She left with Officer Young, and Mason looked at Landon. He was grinning, but it didn't quell the feeling in his belly that he'd fucked up. But when Mason asked him, Landon told him it was fine, he was in his corner. Whatever the hell that meant.

It took Darin and him about two hours to finish up in the barn. Jace was with Logan in the other part of the ranch, taking the calves from their moms. They'd have to go to market soon if this kept up, and it would be their first selling trip rather than buying. Having a herd too big was just as bad as having one that was too small.

Landon was going to bring over three of his bulls to help out. At that rate they'd have calves in a few months to replace the ones that were getting too old to milk. As in the past they would donate a couple to the local food bank, and they'd sell them off to the highest bidder to make some extra money for the food banks. Aunt Georgie was making arrangements for that now.

Landon told him he needed to talk to him about something as well. "I want you to take over the running of the ranch. My ranch. I'm going to take Katie on a trip, and we're going to be gone for a while."

"I can help you out with that." Landon shook his head. "You want me to help whoever you choose. Okay, I get it. And I'll gladly do that as well."

"No. I want you to take my ranch." Mason just stared at him, thinking he had to have heard him wrong. "I'm not...let me start again. You and Emma are going to be married soon, and you're the best man I've ever met in terms of taking care of her. Not that she can't do well on her own, but having you in her corner is going to keep her safe. I am giving you the ranch. Call it a wedding present."

"I can't do that." Landon told him he could. "No. I can't. I can run things for you, but I don't think I can run a ranch the size of yours."

"You won't have to run it, Mason. You'll be the owner. You tell others to do what you want done and they do it. Now, I'm already talking with my attorney and I've had a long talk with my Emma. This thing with you messing up won't be a problem, she'll see...."

"I messed up?" He nodded at him. "You mean about the mayor thing? I was desperate and...shit. I messed up. I was...shit. Shit. Shit."

"Yeah, that's about right." Landon laughed as he patted him on the back. "You're never going to be perfect, son, but you can make it up to her by taking the wind right out of her sails as soon as you see her. Tell her you were an idiot and she'll not know how to handle that." Mason nodded.

"I asked her to marry me this morning, but we never got around to me giving her the ring." Landon fished in his pocket and handed him a small box. "I can't have you buying me her ring. I got her one. It's not much, but I got it for her."

"It was her grandmother's. Katie told me to give it to you last week. Had it on me when I was...when Dirk hit me. I'm powerful glad that he didn't find it. Would have broken my heart to see what he might have done to it." Mason opened the box. "Pretty, isn't it? I think her first husband might have given it to her, and she told me once that he had it made for her. Don't know, I was a might young when she told me."

It wasn't a diamond like he'd thought it would be but a beautiful sapphire. It was surrounded by little pearls that seemed to be blue one second and white the next. The band was wide and had been inlaid with small gems that were as smooth as the ring itself. He could see the inscription, but didn't know what it said. He asked Landon.

"It's French. It says *mon seul et unique amour,* or my one and only love. You can probably have it rescripted if you want, but I kinda like it." So did Mason. "She's a good girl, my Emma, and what you don't get from me when we sign the papers, you will from her. And if you'd be able to talk her into a baby or two before I leave this world, well, her mom would be tickled pink."

"And you? Will you be happy with having children that are not wholly human?" Landon smacked him in the

146

head with his palm. "I had to ask. You do know that they'll be like me for the most part."

"I'm hoping they'll be like you both. Stubborn to no end, smart as tacks, and rich beyond what I'm giving you now." He asked him what Dirk was going to say. "At this point...we talked it over, me and Katie, and we can't have him...he's done. I don't want to say I don't have a son, but I'm thinking if he don't get him some help soon, it's not gonna end well for him."

Landon hugged him, and Mason hugged him back. He was glad that he was better. He might have missed him more than he'd thought. When he saw Emma walking toward them, Landon told him good luck and moved away to enter the barn behind him. Emma was nearly to him when he dropped to one knee in front of her.

"I'm a fool. And an idiot. I shouldn't have thrown you under the bus like I did. But I was so afraid that they'd be able to convince me to take the job and that I'd really fuck it up that I just panicked. I'm sorry. So very sorry." He lifted the little box to her and let her see what was inside. "Your father said this was your grandmothers and that you were to have it. Katie thought it would be nice for you to be asked—"

"Where's the one you bought me?" He looked up at her. "This morning you said you have me a ring. I'd like to see it."

Her voice was all wrong for someone who was being asked to be married, but he dug the little box out of his pocket. In comparison, his was cheap and dime store looking. But it was all he could afford, and he had been really proud that he'd done it.

"Ask me again." Mason asked her what she meant. "To marry you. I love my grandmother's ring and I'll wear it, but not on the finger you are to give me a ring on. That one is for the one you bought me."

"Will you marry me, Emma McBride? I love you. I'm a screw-up. A lowly rancher with not much…I didn't have much in the way of offering you something. But your father said that he was…never mind. Will you marry me? Have babies with me and make me the happiest man in the world?" He looked up at her when she didn't answer right away. "Emma?"

"Will you change me? I mean soon? I want to be able to run with you. Shift and be a cat with you. Protect you when you need me to." He nodded. "Then yes, I'll marry you, but if you ever do that to me again, you'll be very sorry."

"I already am." He took the ring out of the box and slipped it on her finger. "I think the other one suits you more."

"No, this one is perfect because you gave it to me. I love the other one, as I said, but this is from your heart, and I love it more." Mason put the other ring on her other hand and kissed her. "How soon?"

"I have to get a license, and we have to have some kind of test. Not sure what that's all about, but—" She put her hand over his mouth and said how long before he could change her. "Oh. I'll have to talk to Jace. He's done it before, so he'll have first-hand info. You really want it now? I heard it was really painful."

"I want to be like you in all ways." Mason kissed her again, this time holding her body to his for several minutes. When he put her down, she stepped back. "Thanks to you, I have to make a few phone calls and take on a job that I've never done before. Plus, I have to call my boss. He might not be happy to find out that I'm well enough to come back to work and now have a temporary job."

"Then quit and be the mayor. You'd do a great job, and you'd be right here with me all the time." She shook her head, but he could see the desire there. "You'd be Mayor Douglas, and I'd be fucking you on that big desk of yours whenever I'm in town."

"You're not going to get me to do this with sex." He wiggled his brows at her, and she laughed. "You're not right in the head. I'm leaving. I'll see you later."

CHAPTER 11

Dirk walked around the house three times and knocked on every window and door. There just wasn't anyone there. Not a servant nor his family. And he was getting madder by the minute. When someone spoke behind him, he turned to see a big man with a gun, but he seemed to be alone.

"You're trespassing." Dirk opened his mouth to tell him who he was, but the man raised his hand. "I know who you are, but you're still not allowed to be here. Now, I've called the cops and they're on their way. So you just sit that ass of yours down there and be a good boy."

"I'm Dirk McBride, you motherfucker, and I have more right to be here than you do." Dirk reached for his gun, but the man raised his first. "You shoot me and there will be hell to pay. If you live long enough to make it to jail."

"You're a little shit, aren't you? Mason said you were a little on the odd side, but you're really off your cork if you think that...you really are something else." Dirk didn't think he meant that in a good way and said nothing. "Now I'm going to come close enough to get that gun from you. Then we're going to wait on the cops."

The man moved quicker than he could see. And when he blinked again, his gun was in the front of the other man's pants, as well as the knife that he'd had in his pocket. Dirk wanted to attack the man, but wasn't ready to do that just yet and stood there.

"How much do you want?" The man asked him what he meant. "Money. How much do you want to let me go? I have a lot of it, and as soon as I get into the house, I'll give it to you. I'm a very wealthy man. The McBrides have more money than anyone, and it'll all be mine soon."

"From what I've heard, you have shit. Less than shit, and a murderer doesn't usually have the means to any money so far as I know." Dirk just waved him off. "You saying you didn't murder anyone?"

"When people get in my way, I take care of things. And with my connections, I'm not going to go to jail. My sister is supposed to be this great attorney, and when she finds out that I'm being arrested, she's going to take care of me." The man snorted. "You just don't know the power of money, that's all. You have no idea the kind of power that I can use. I'm a very wealthy man."

"So you keep telling me." The man looked to his left, and so did Dirk. There was nothing there, but the man looked at him again. "They're coming for you. And a pretty boy like you, you'll be butt fucked before the end of the day, I'm betting."

"I'm not gay." The man just laughed. "Don't laugh at me. I'm not trying to be funny. Stop laughing."

But he continued. And not only did he laugh, but harder and louder. Dirk had enough. People just did not treat him like he was common. He cleared the distance between him and the man in no time and knocked him back. Dirk was ready to pound his head into the ground when he noticed that he was not moving. Not only that, but he was bleeding from the head too.

Dirk could hear the sirens now. The dumbass really had called the cops. What the hell was wrong with people? Didn't they care that he was a McBride and that his kind didn't go to jail? He grabbed the man's wallet, his guns, and his knife back and was ready to put a bullet in his head when he heard doors slamming. Dirk took off to the woods instead of getting rid of the trash that had the nerve to try and have him arrested.

Dirk stayed just within the trees to see what was going on. He wasn't afraid of going to jail. At most he'd spend a few hours there, and then Emma would have him out on bail that his dad would pay. It was the fact that they all seemed to think he'd done something wrong when it had been him that had been wronged.

For weeks now he'd been trying to figure out what had happened to the people in his family. The only thing he could think of was Mason. The lowlife had been messing with their minds and turning them against him. Dirk had really liked the way things had been, and the sooner they got back with the program, the better he'd like it.

He pulled the list that his father had given him out of his pocket. He'd finally gotten around to really looking at it, and had to laugh every time he saw it. Get a job was the first thing on the long list, and the second one was to get a place to live. Dirk had one, and he'd be living there for the rest of his life too if his family would just remember who he was.

Dirk had had some issues with that for some time as well. The peons of the town were acting like he was nothing and that his name was nothing as well. He was Dirk McBride, and the sooner they started to remember that and his station in life, the better off they'd be.

When the cops started to the woods in the opposite direction he was, Dirk made his way to the road again. They were so stupid if they thought he'd just wait there for them. First of all, he had to find his family, and then there was going to be hell to pay. What the fuck did they think they were doing treating him this way?

Dirk knew that he was special. He was good looking if he did say so himself. And he took a great deal of pride in his attire. His knowledge of fashion was second to none, and he prided himself on being up to date on all the seasonal changes as well.

Money had never meant anything to him other than the fact that he liked to spend it. Dirk couldn't remember the last time he'd even looked at a price tag or, for that matter, a bill. Just hand what he wanted to the girl at the counter, sign his name, and be on his way. Getting what he wanted was a priority to him. As it should be.

McBride had been a household name for as long as he'd been able to remember. His father didn't seem to get that. His mom was stupid about fashion and he had to take her to task on more than one occasion about what she was wearing. Of course, she'd never paid him any mind, but when she was dumb enough not dress in a way that was befitting to him and his good name, Dirk would just leave her. It would piss off his dad, but he had a reputation to uphold and she was really not with it.

His dad was a different matter altogether. Why he felt he had to go out in the fields every day was just beyond Dirk. To him it was what you paid people for. Do the shit work and let you rake in the money. And his dad did make a lot of it too. About a year ago it had been in some magazine that his dad, him too, as he was his only son, was one of the top five richest people in the world. Dirk smiled.

He'd gone out and celebrated his good fortune by spending a great deal of money, and if he remembered correctly, he'd been put in jail for something. One call to Emma had taken care of that. Now that was changed too.

When he got back to his house, he went in through the back door and sat in the kitchen. Last night the woman had started to smell up the house, so he'd put her in the dumpster and set her to the curb. He had no idea when the trash was picked up, but having her smell out of his house had made vast improvements. Still, there was little to eat now and he had no more money.

The television in the kitchen no longer worked, and that really pissed him off that he couldn't have it replaced. Going to his list, he wrote that down as well. When his family took him back in, he was going to show them that he'd been thinking about them and what they could do to improve his life. There were perhaps forty things on his list, and Dirk was quite proud of some of them.

The house was something that he'd had to really think about. He wanted his own. And servants to clean up after him as well. Plus the cook and someone to make sure he had an endless supply of drugs and wine. Dirk had been without a hit for a while now and wasn't really concerned about it. He didn't do it that much, preferring alcohol over drugs every time. But if he did want drugs, he wanted them there where he didn't have to go out and find someone to sell them to him.

The house, as he'd stated above, would be clean too. No more having the servants skip his room because he was in the room. He'd decided that having three bedrooms was convenient, as he could have each of them filled with all his things he could move from room to room. He'd never have to sleep in a mess that they'd been too lazy to see.

His father never used the limo service anymore, and he wanted those privileges put back in place. If there was trouble with it, then his dad would have to take care of it. Keeping track of his own car was just too much work. A limo would save him so much time finding a place to park too.

There would be no more talk about him finding a job. He had one. It was simply being who he was. If anyone thought that he just got out of bed and looked like he did, then they had no business being a part of his clique. It took him time to look this good and money to make it work.

That was another thing. It had taken him the longest to figure out just how much he wanted in allowance each week. He'd really thought that a thousand would be enough, but when he thought about things, the parties he wanted to go to, the gifts he wanted to buy for himself, he knew it was going to have to be way more than that. He thought about five grand a week, then just wrote down an endless supply in the form of his own bank account. His dad could just keep it tapped off and he'd use it as he saw fit. Also, a separate credit card to use when he was short on cash. Then there were the last three things on his list.

His sister wasn't to marry beneath her. Maybe she did have a job and worked for a living, but she was a McBride and had to keep up the blueblood line. She could fuck Mason if she wanted, but there would be no marriage and certainly no brats. He had a list of candidates on the other page of people he felt that she should consider.

His mom was going to have her body redone. A face lift wasn't enough. She was sagging everywhere, and it was just too embarrassing for her to be out in public, especially when she told people who she was. Dirk also had a name of a good doctor that could take forty years off herself, and she'd be good enough to be seen with him. A fashion stylist was also on his list, but that was a given. His family was going to start looking like him, a McBride.

Dad. What do to with Dad had been the hardest to figure out. Dirk had thought of all kinds of things to do with him. Have him get a lift and tuck too, but he'd never do it not even if Dirk tried to explain to him that he had to look good to be seen with him. And there was him working. Dad would not quit that either. Smelling like a horse seemed to be like a cologne to him. No, this called for bigger things.

"Dad will have to be put away." It would be easy too. His dad was old, and Dirk had figured all he had to do was to have his dad stand before the judge and tell them what he did all day. Then Dirk would stand beside him. It would be difficult, but he'd do it for the sake of their family name and show the judge what he had to work with. Dirk had no doubt that his dad would be in a home in moments, and no longer a social problem for him.

He looked at his other list, his things to do to get his family with the program of getting him back in the house. Today had been the day that he'd confront them, but that hadn't gone well at all. Dirk had it on his list to call the police and have them make his parents take him back, but that was third on his list. Tomorrow he was going to go and see Emma at her job. Things were going to be complete by tomorrow night, and he'd be in his own bed. Smiling, he sat down in front of the tiny television that he'd brought down from the bedroom and turned it on. This woman should have made better plans for having his kind come and see her. This shit was for the birds.

~~~

157

"Why don't you take the job?" Emma looked at Mr. Patterson, her boss. "You'd be better off there than here. Things are changing here that, frankly, might make me leave as well."

Emma didn't say anything. She wasn't even sure what to say to him. She loved her job and everything about it...the way things worked to a conclusion nearly every time. Then there was the way she felt when she closed a case that she'd won.

She'd been asked to go and see him by Mr. Foster, the firm's president. She had no idea why, but she'd done as he'd asked. The only thing she'd been told to do was to wear the little body camera and just to tell him what she had planned.

"Don't you like being a lawyer?" Patterson told her the only thing he liked was the check. "That's really sad. I mean, you went to college for all that time just to draw a check. I love what I do. The money is only secondary."

"Yeah, because you have it all." Emma shifted on her chair. She never discussed her family or their wealth. She supposed that if someone wanted to know they'd only have to look her up, but it was something that rarely came up. "I mean, if I had all the money you had, I'd be sitting on my ass too. The mayoral position would be perfect. If they give you any grief, then just buy them off."

"I'd never do that." Patterson snorted at her. "I wouldn't. And the reason I'm here is just what I said. I'd like permission from the company to help out a little until they get someone to replace me. It would only be for a short time, and I'd still be able to work here too."

"Did you know that Foster really likes you?" Emma said she liked him too. "No, I mean really likes you. I've been asking around, and I think he'd screw you if you let him. Might make you a better check come bonus time."

Emma stood up, and Patterson just laughed at her. "You're going to take that back and stop asking such questions. I don't sleep with the bosses to get where I am, and I have no intentions of ever doing so."

"Yeah, I know. Don't think I haven't hinted enough for you to fuck me." Emma sat down, stunned. "You have no idea how many times I've tried to get you cornered, but you were just clueless. I've figured out that you're either a dyke or you just don't like me. And I think it's both. Are you a pussy eater, Emma?"

This time when she stood up, he did as well. Her temper was hot right now and she could feel Mason right there. If he was talking to her, she had no clue what he was saying because her mind was running through all the things she'd like to say to this man. When she picked up her purse, he came around the table to her and grabbed her arms.

"Don't touch me." He just laughed and shoved her back in the chair. When he leaned against the desk and stared at her, Emma started to stand again.

"Sit there and shut up. I'm going to let you suck my dick. Then I'm going to tell Foster that you're leaving. When you do, you're going to never say a fucking word. I figure I'm about done here anyway, and might as well have something that I've wanted for a long time." When he reached for his belt, she punched him in the cock. He bent over, and when he did, she stood up and kneed him in the face. The door opened behind her, and she turned, fists up.

"Don't, baby, it's me." She had to take several deep breaths while her vision cleared. When Mason pulled her into his arms, she let him hold her, but her temper was still on the edge. "Don't kill him. He's not worth it."

"Do you know what he said to me?" He told her he'd been in Foster's office. "What the hell was that all about? I was bait?"

"Yes, and Mr. Foster is going to apologize profusely as soon as he can move." She looked up at Mason and asked him what he meant. "I hurt him. Not as badly as I wanted, but he's going to think twice before he asks you to do something like this again."

"He wanted him to try this." Mason said she was right, but Foster had figured that when things got bad, he'd call security. "That's just not right. I mean, what if he'd hurt me? And what…I hit him."

The man in question hadn't moved since she'd hit him with his name plate. When he'd been going down, she'd touched it and picked it up. Just as Patterson reached for her again, she'd hit him. This time he didn't move.

"We're going to go home and in a few days you can come back here and talk to him again." She shook her head. "Honey, I don't think he's going to be able to talk to you for a couple of days at least. When he wouldn't tell me which office you were in, I sort of let my cat come out a little and we had some fun. Would you believe that he spoke right up just before I hit him again?"

"I'm just betting he did. But I'm not working for a man who could do this to one of his partners." The door opened behind them and Emma felt her body being slid behind Mason's. He was big enough that she couldn't see who it was, but when Mr. Foster spoke, she peeked around Mason at him.

"I want to talk to you about what just happened." Emma stood beside Mason and glared at her boss. "It's not what you think. I've been hearing things he's been saying for weeks now, and when you left, things just got worse. I had to catch him in the act."

"With this?" Mason held something in his hand and Foster nodded. "You're not getting this back until she says you can have it. And as for your little trick here, if I ever hear even a hint of you pulling this sort of shit again, I will come back here and tear you apart."

"I'll need that in the event that Patterson sues us." Mason handed her the little thumb drive, and she looked at it for several seconds while Mr. Foster explained what was on it. "I've been recording all kinds of things around here that he's been doing. And if he tries to take me to court—not that I think he'll win, but if he does—then—"

"I'm suing you." Mr. Foster just stared at her. "I will give you my formal resignation and then I'm going to sue you. This recording will be posted on every website that I can think of, too. What you did wasn't just illegal, but it was unethical as well as immoral. To think that I came here in good faith to tell you that I was going to come back on Monday. And you pull this shit."

"I've made you partner." Emma only reached for her purse in lieu of answering him. "You can't just walk out on me, Emma. I've been thinking of all the cases we can take on once we clean house here. We'll be millionaires in no time."

"Mason, call the police. And an ambulance please." She went to the other side of the desk and placed a call. "Hello, Margaret…yes, I'm back for right now. Mr. Foster has just made some very…yes, I guess you have seen it. Could you please make sure that…you're a doll, and I'll have Fox make you some of those cookies that you like and have them brought to you. Yes, I think I can arrange it so that he brings them to you too."

"You can't just have her give you copies of security tapes." Emma said nothing and took Mason's hand. "Emma, think what you're doing. No one in this state will want to use us again if this gets out. I can't allow you to do this."

"I did nothing. You did when you asked me to put on a wire and camera and come in here and let that piece of shit make a pass at me." Emma felt her temper rise again, and when Mason put his arm around her, she calmed. "You're very lucky my husband came in here with me, or so help me, I would have beaten the shit out of you too."

After stopping by the security office, she and Mason left the building. Emma was shaking so hard that he had to hold her before they got very far. Now that she'd dealt with the issue, she was hurt. Mr. Foster had actually used her as bait. She looked over at Mason as he drove them back to the house.

"Do you suppose we can find a justice of the peace and get this finished?" He looked at her when he stopped at the light. "I want to be your wife now, Mason. Right now."

"All right, but your parents aren't going to be too happy with you about running off." She told him she'd call them when it was done. Mason pulled up in front of the court house and turned to look at her. "Gerard is in town, right down the road. And I think that Holly is here as well. Will they do as witnesses?"

"Yes. Perfect." He was moving up the steps with her when she realized that he could contact them like he talked to her. "And when we get home after you ravish me, I want you to convert me. Tonight. The thought of being a cat and being able to tear someone's throat out really appeals to me."

"Whoa, baby. We'll have to work up to that. Let's just get you married to me. Then we'll talk about your anger issues." Gerard came in behind them with Jace and Holly. Forty minutes later, she was saying yes to him and well on her way to being Emma Douglas. After the afternoon she'd had, this was a perfect ending to it all.

CHAPTER 12

Mason had a wife. It was all that was going through his mind at any given second of the day. Not only did he have a lovely wife that he loved more than anything in the world, but he was the owner of one of the largest, if not the largest ranches in the state. Mason looked at Jace when he snapped his fingers in front of him.

"Are you listening?" He shook his head no. "Well, you'd better. This has gone way beyond a spoiled man taking his revenge out on his mom and dad. Dirk has killed a few people. And hurt a great many more. One of them being a friend of mine."

"I had heard about Mark. He's going to be all right, isn't he?" Jace said that once he shifted he was fine, but it had taken a lot out of him to be hurt in the head that way. "I'm so sorry. I'm paying attention now."

"We're going to set up a way for him to get into the house. That seems to be his biggest thing right now. That and money. Did you know that he refers to himself as Dirk McBride? Not me or anything like that, but as his name? What a fucking moron." Jace moved some of the papers around on this desk before handing him some of them. "That's where he's been staying, we think. LeBlanc said that someone from the trash company called his office this morning with a report of a body in a trash dumpster. She'd been dead for a few days and he'd put her out to the curb. This guy is really making a name for himself."

Sadie James had been eighty-four years old when she'd been murdered. Blunt force trauma to her head had killed her. The report that Mason was looking at said that the house had been ransacked and trashed, as well as any valuables that she might have had were gone. There was also no money in her purse, something that her neighbors said she had on her at all times.

"Not that I don't believe you, but how do they know it was him?" Jace said that the place was covered in his prints, and even the rolling pin that he'd used to hit her had his prints on it. "What was he doing in her home?"

"LeBlanc said that it looked to him like he was living there. He said it would explain why they'd not been able to find him. And her car wasn't used, so he's either got one stashed somewhere or he's walking."

"Was it a standard?" Both he and Jace stood up when Emma came into the room. She waved them both to have a seat and asked again. "The reason I ask is because he's never been able to drive one. I think it was just laziness on his part, but he never learned."

"Yeah, it says here that it was a standard." Mason kissed her before continuing with the plan. "We're trying to get him to come to us, sort of. Jace thinks, along with LeBlanc, that he'll go to the house on the idea that your family is taking him back in."

Holly joined them, talking as she entered the room. "I've done some research on the law firm of yours, and you are well rid of them. And so you know, Ed, the family attorney, is going to go after them for you. I guess he's had some issues with them before. That guy Foster? He gives the appearance of being this really dopey kind of fatherly like, but he's a prick."

Emma nodded. Mason had had to hold Emma back from returning and murdering the man, but Holly told her that she had a better plan. The two of them, along with Palmer, had been closed up in the study all morning. He told her whatever she wanted to do was completely up to her.

"Oh, you should know that I've taken the mayoral position as of this morning." Mason just smiled at her. "You knew I would, so don't look all pleased with yourself. It might get you hurt later."

"I hope so." She playfully punched him in the arm, and he turned back to his brother. "This plan to get Dirk to the house, what then? I mean, once he's there, what is going to happen?"

"I'm going to have him arrested. I mean...sort of." Mason looked at Jace, then at Landon when he came into the room to join in on the conversation. "He's going to try and hurt me, and I'm going to take him down."

"You're not going to let him try to hurt you." Katie told Landon to sit down and behave before she looked at Mason. "He's mad at you mostly. I just spoke to him. And before any of you start yelling at me, that nice man Ed recorded it all. Apparently, Mason, you're the bane of his very life, and he wants you out of the picture. He's most upset, too, that you and Emma are married. I hung up when I could no longer stand his mouth."

He figured that once the paper came out today that he'd be getting a few calls. When Emma had called her parents after the short ceremony, her dad could be heard whooping it up all the way through the phone. When he'd talked to him, Landon could barely contain his happiness and told him he'd talk to him later. Katie told him she was very proud of him, but to expect a second wedding with all the fanfare later.

"So we get him to the house. I'm assuming that the police will be there as well?" Jace nodded, and told him that the SWAT team was also going to be there in the event that something went wrong. "A lot can go wrong, you know. Not just with him trying to hurt his father, but didn't I hear that he had a gun or two? We have to figure that he might try to kill him, not just hurt him."

"I'd like to address that if I may." Everyone looked at Aunt Georgie. "I'm not going to say that I like this plan, but I think that sending in a human is going to get someone killed. I think, since he's already mad at Mason, that he'd be the best one to confront him. I don't want anyone hurt, but Mason is a good deal better able to handle it than you are, Landon."

"I like that plan." Katie looked at him. "I know that I'm asking a great deal of you, but like your aunt said, it would be easier for you to come back from him shooting you."

"Mother? I don't want either of them hurt, but sheesh, let's be a little conscious of the fact that I just married him." Emma looked at her mom, then at Mason. "You can't get yourself killed. I'm your wife now, and I forbid it."

"All right, love, no dying. But you have to agree, Aunt Georgie is right." He pulled Emma into his arms. "I can smell silver if he should have some on him, and I'm quicker than your dad is, even though he is feeling better. If he tries to shoot me, I have a good chance of getting away before he can do much."

"Do I get to say anything about this?" Landon looked like a hurt child, and Mason just barely held his humor in.

"I'm an old man, not to mention the father of the little shit. If anyone should be there, it should be me."

"And what do I do if this time he kills you? Huh?" Katie poked Landon in the chest as she yelled at him. "I can't do that again, you old turd. I need you. And I've already picked out some of my clothes to take on this trip we're planning. I want to see Europe with you, and take a cruise. You'll be there or so help me, I'll…I'll stuff you and take you along just so I don't have to be alone."

Landon held his sobbing wife. She begged him over and over to let Mason do it, and Mason thought he was going to tell her no. But in the end Landon gave in, but he said that he'd like to talk to his son once it was over. Everyone agreed that if it was possible he could.

The plan was good. And solid. Mason was going to go to the house early in the morning. His brothers and a few of their friends were going to be there as well…two inside, the rest of them all over the property. They would keep each other updated on where Dirk was at all times. Aunt Georgie and Katie were going to be at Aunt Georgie's house with the police. LeBlanc had okayed that they do this their way to a point, but if things went sour, he was going in full force. The police and the SWAT team were going to wait until LeBlanc said it was okay to go in and everything was being recorded.

Now that they had a way of contacting Dirk—the phone being set up for him at the mall had been Katie's idea—they could contact him at any time once things were complete. Katie said that Dirk had told her over and over that she should have thought of that sooner, and she'd had to bite her tongue to tell him she'd not wanted to talk to him after he'd nearly killed his father. The phone wasn't up to his standards either, apparently.

Katie told them that he'd complained about it not being what he'd had before. How was he to use it in front of his friends should he need to make a call? And there wasn't a good camera that he could take pictures of his clothing to keep for future style issues. Everything about the phone had been subpar.

Landon was set to call Dirk at five o'clock in the morning, Dirk's usual bed time, and tell him to go to the house, that he and Katie had a change of heart about things. Mason was going to be there waiting in the event that he was closer than they thought. LeBlanc had admitted that he'd lost him twice since he'd been following him after leaving the mall.

"He just blends in. Not with the people—no, not even close—but going in and out of shops. He must know them better than I do my own house." Katie said he more than likely did. "I just gave up following him and had a man put in all the posh stores around town. He might not have any money to spend, but he sure window shops more than my sister."

Once he received the call and was headed to the house, then the department of men would go along with him—out of the way, of course—and keep an eye on him. It had been Holly's idea to send a limo for Dirk so that he could be contained better. But an officer was going to be driving it should something happen.

At six thirty in the morning, after trying for an hour to contact his son, Landon called and told him that it was set up. He was going to come out to the house around five-thirty that night, and Landon had told him that the car would be there to get him. Dirk was going to be at the mall. He wanted to make a list of things that he was going to purchase when he returned with money and cards.

"He gave me a list, Mason. A list of…I guess you could call them demands. And he wants to have his mom…he wants her to be altered. Sent to a specialist to have her face lifted and her body toned." Mason asked him if he had a reason for that. "Yeah, he said that if she was going to go out and claim to be a McBride, then she had to suit him. He had a public image to maintain, and they were going to expect nothing but the best. When I asked him what he had planned for me, you know what the little shit said?"

"I have no idea. I wouldn't think he'd want you to go under the knife. You're much too tough, and I think you both look good the way you are." Landon snorted, but Mason knew he was hurt. "What are his big plans for you?"

"He's going to have me put in a nursing home. Changing my name, of course. He doesn't want anyone to know that we're related." Mason wanted to go and find the fuck right now and show him how badly he'd hurt his dad this time. "I don't even…what the hell am I supposed to say to him? And he said that a judge would be on his side because, and I quote, 'there is no way that we could be of the same mold.' He's damned well got that right."

At four o'clock, Mason and Landon went to the house. Emma was there as well, but she'd promised to stay out of sight with her dad. Mason hadn't wanted either of them there in the event that Dirk started spouting out more of his demands, but Landon wanted to talk to his son, and Emma wanted to make sure they were both safe. By five fifteen, the limo was leaving the mall and had the little shit in the back. Things were about to be finished.

~~~

Dirk felt good. He was going to go home and clean things up, and let them get back to normal. Well, as normal as it could be from now on. And his dad had been very

171

receptive to his changes too. Dirk thought that was going to go so much easier on them when he told them the rest of his plans.

He'd seen the paper this morning announcing the marriage of his sister to Mason. That had to be taken care of first. There was no way that man was going to be a part of his elite family. There were going to be higher standards now, and if he had to break a few heads for it to be the way he wanted it, the way it should have been from the beginning, then so be it. Dirk referred to his list.

Last night he'd gone over it and numbered it in order of importance. It had taken him nearly an hour to get the first one chosen. There had been so many things that he wanted to do first that he'd had to really work on it. First and foremost had been getting his money taken care of. Then he'd seen the headlines in the paper and had to move everything back down one. But money and his establishment into being in charge had to be at the top. No more fucking around.

When the car slid to a stop, he nearly told the driver he was fired. The man, for sure, would never drive him around the way he jerked him to a stop at every chance he got. He'd just have to make sure that he was fired after his father and he talked. The man might have to take his dad to the home today, and if he fired him now, then they'd have to prolong the wait to get it over with.

Fox was still there. Dirk had nothing to give him, so he just waited for him to speak first. The sooner they figured out who was in charge around here the better. Of course, Fox had to go. He'd not want any of the old staff here once he was really in charge. As Fox led him to the living room, Dirk thought of all the changes he was going to make in the house too.

New furniture was going to be a biggy. A bigger television set in the living room and his room. There would be a gaming room too, something his father had refused to let him have before now. And there would be more staff, pretty girls that would fawn all over him when he needed a boost to his ego. That wasn't often, but he wanted it and could afford it, so that was going to happen.

When he entered the living room, Mason was standing near the fireplace and his father wasn't there.

"What's the meaning of this?" Dirk turned to ask Fox, but the bastard was gone. Dirk looked at Mason. "Where is my dad, and what the fuck are you doing here?"

"I've come to talk to you." Dirk turned to leave, but Mason's next words made him pause. "You leave and you'll get nothing. Not one thin dime, and certainly not a place to live."

Dirk would only tolerate so much, and he'd give this man his due when the time was right. For now he was married to his sister. He went into the living room and sat on the couch, right in the middle so as not to look as if he wanted Mason to join him. And if he did sit with him, the couch would be burned with the rest of the household furniture.

"Well?" Dirk hated this man more than anyone he'd ever hated. In school the Douglas boys had always had women with them despite their lack of good clothing and modes of transportation. And they were smart, too, even though none of them had gone to college.

"You've been a very bad man, haven't you, Dirk?" Dirk had no idea what he was talking about and said as much. "You've been on a murdering spree that has the police looking everywhere for you. What do you have to say for yourself?"

173

"About what?" Mason said nothing but stood up straighter against the mantel. "I've done a few things that anyone would have done to get to where I am. So what if a few people lost their lives? My sister is going to get me off and if she can't, Dad will pay them off. It's the way the rich do things. And since I'm Dirk McBride, things get done for me."

"My wife isn't going to help you. She's got a good job now, and helping you isn't part of the equation." Dirk started to stand up and argue, but Mason was taller and that wasn't good. "You should also know that being Dirk anyone isn't going to cut it when you go to trial."

"I'm glad you brought up Emma. She's going to have to leave you. I won't have her married to someone like you." Mason asked him what kind of person he thought he was. "Let's face it, Mason, you're just not up to standards with us. You're a rancher, for Christ's sake. I just won't have you bringing down our bloodline with your tainted blood. Emma will listen to me or she'll be taken care of, like I'm going to take care of a few other things around here now that I'm back."

Mason laughed. And for a few minutes too. Dirk wanted to get up and hit him, but he didn't. Then he remembered that he had a gun and pulled it out, telling Mason to shut the fuck up.

"You going to shoot me, Dirk? I would strongly advise that you not. Not only will you piss me off, but I might hurt you badly should you try." Dirk was tempted to show him that he was going to do it and right now, but paused. "Your dad wants to talk to you."

"It's about fucking time. On your way out, tell him I'm ready to see him now." Mason laughed again. "You should learn to listen to your betters, Mason. I'm sure you'll get along better in life if you simply know where your station is."

"My station? I'll tell you what my station is, you little shit. I'm married to your sister. And we're happily in love. You, you little fuck, are not going to come between us or even have a say in anything that we do. As of right now, I'm the one allowing you to be here, I'm the one that is keeping the police at bay, and you, sir, should be grateful that I'm not allowed to fucking kill you."

"Kill me? You think you can kill me?" The gun was pointed at Mason again, and the man paused. "Good, now I want you to tell my dad to get his ass in here so I can get started on the things I need to get done."

"You put the gun on the table and he'll come in here with us." Dirk said no. "Then I'll make a call, bring in the police, and have you arrested. It's that simple."

Dirk wasn't going to jail. He might be delayed in getting things done, but there was no way that he was going to go to jail. He had money and connections. His sister might be mad at him, but she'd never let him stay one moment in a cell. Of course, she'd told him he was on his own from now on, but that had been because he'd taken her away from her job when he'd needed her.

But to Dirk, things should be the way he wanted them. All the time. Not just because of who he was, and that was important enough, but because he was rich. Even his sister should know that as the male of the family, he was going to get it all. And while she'd been nice enough to help him, it was her duty to continue to do so. But he needed to get things going.

"If I put my gun here, you'll bring my dad out so I can talk to him? There are things we have to discuss, and the sooner the better." Mason nodded. "How do I know I can trust you? You're not exactly the nicest person I know."

"You're right on that one. Had I been in charge of this crap, you'd be in prison right about now." Dirk laughed and told him that wasn't likely. "You think not? We'll see. Put both guns and the knife on the table and I'll call your dad out."

"Dad is here now?" Mason said nothing. Dirk yelled for his dad several times and got nothing. "You're a liar, Mason. And as soon as I talk to my dad, you're going to regret talking to me at all, much less lying to me."

"I already do." When Mason whistled, his dad came to the doorway. Dirk told him to get in here, that time was being wasted, but his dad just walked away. When Dirk went to get him, Mason was suddenly in front of him. "I told you, guns and knife on the table and he'll talk to you. And if you call me a liar again, I'm going to tear you to pieces."

Dirk stalked back to the table. He slammed the gun he had in his hand on the table, followed quickly by the knife. When Mason only cocked that fucking brow at him again, Dirk reached into the back of his pants and put the second gun there as well. Mason came into the room again, but he didn't go to the fireplace this time but stood near the table. And as if he were magical, the guns and knife were gone.

"What the fuck are you doing? Give those back to me." Mason only sat down and whistled again, this time loudly and longer. Not only did his dad come into the room, but Emma as well. Good, get two things off his list at one time.

His dad sat on the other chair that was opposite to the couch, and Emma sat on Mason's lap. It was disgusting, and he had to look away before he started on her first. His dad had to be dealt with or nothing was going to go right.

"Did you do what I told you?" His dad said nothing but looked at Mason. "I'm the one you're supposed to be talking to, not him. Mason is nothing right now. I'm the one that's important."

"I used to think that as well." His dad sounded sad, more than likely because he had to give him what he wanted. But Dirk was the one with the money, and he had to do something so that the name McBride was no longer sullied. "You're a great disappointment to me, Dirk. I never thought I'd say that to one of my children, but you truly are."

"For what? You're the one that kicked me out. Had you just continued on the way things were, none of this would have happened." He leaned back on the couch. "I asked you a question, Dad, did you do what I told you?"

"No. And I'm not going to either." His dad tossed a blue packet like thing at him. "This is my will. I had them make you a copy as well. As of right now, you're getting nothing should I die. And as much as you'd like that to happen, it's not going to be any time soon. And your mother and I aren't going to be remade in your image either. Emma is going to stay married to Mason and hopefully have me lots of grandchildren. But you, son, are on your own. After today we will not—"

"You can't do this to me. I'm your son. The heir of your money. And I want it. I've grown to love having it. Now...." Dirk turned to Emma. "Get off him. Christ, and you change his will right fucking now. I don't know how you thought this was going to work, but I'm not going to stand for you treating me this way any longer. Get me my cards and money and I'll pretend that you didn't just tell me no."

"I should have told you no a lot more. Perhaps this might have ended better." Emma stood up, but she didn't move away from Mason as Dad continued speaking. "I'm ashamed of what you've been doing. You killed those people, Dirk. Don't you even care?"

"Pay them off. It's about all you're good for. And I had to do what I needed to do. You threw me out in the streets. You took all my money. For what? A lesson? Well, the only thing I learned was not to trust you again. That's why I'm putting my foot down and having things my way." Dirk looked at Emma. "You are the one who should be ashamed. Christ, you're married to a...a Douglas. What the fuck are you thinking? Well, you'll fix that too. And pay him off to never mention his association with my name again. I'm Dirk McBride, and I'm in charge now."

"You're a moron." Dirk looked at Mason when he called him a name. "A complete and total moron if you think even one thing that you're spewing is going to happen."

Mason nodded to Emma, and she went to the phone. If he had the gun right now, he'd have shot her. Instead he started for her, and was stopped when Mason picked him up by his throat.

Clawing at his neck to try and get Mason's hands off him, he stared at the man. How dare he touch him? Dirk wasn't going to put up with this any longer. When he was tossed away, he stood up and straightened his clothing and glared. His throat was sore, and his neck hurt, but there was no way he'd let this bastard win this round.

"You're going to pay for that." Mason only laughed, and he heard the sirens screaming in the drive. "The police. Perfect. I do hope you have everything in order, Mason. You're going away for a very long time."

"Me?" He laughed again. "You should really think about who they're here to arrest, Dirk the Dick. I'm pretty sure that it's not going to be me led away. And you'll be rotting in prison too before anyone comes to help you."

The police came into the room with their guns drawn. Dirk watched them go to Mason, and he smiled. His point was proven when two more went to his dad. But when he was jerked up from the couch that he'd just sat down on, Dirk turned to the man to see what the hell he was doing.

"Dirk Dwight McBride, you're under arrest for the murder of Sadie James, Michael Lowendick, and the attempted murder of your father, Landon Dwight McBride, and Mark Coldwell." Dirk tried to get away but the cuffs were on him before he could take a step. "Would you like for me to add resisting arrest to your list?"

"Emma, tell this man to unhand me." She only stood there holding onto Mason. "Emma, this is just stupid. Tell them to let me go and we'll just get finished with what we were talking about. You can't mean to teach me another lesson. I'm sick to death of what you think I need to learn. Tell them who I am, goddamn it."

"He's Dirk McBride." Dirk smiled at her and looked at the officer holding him, waiting for him to let him go. "And there are three more names you can add to that list of murdered people. I'll have the files sent to your office in the morning."

Dirk tried his best to get away, but all he managed to do was get himself dragged to the back of the cruiser and shoved in. People were going to pay for his treatment, and he was going to start with his sister. Screaming at them to let him go resulted in one of the officers turning around and hitting him in the face. It was the last thing he remembered for a while.

CHAPTER 13

Emma sat at the desk she'd been given and stared at nothing. She supposed she should get something done before they came in and told her she was fired, but for the life of her she just didn't have the energy. Her brother was going to prison and she'd covered up three other deaths he'd committed. When someone knocked on her door, she looked up at Georgie and bid her to come in.

"How you settling in?"

Emma told her she was doing fine, but noticed that there were still packages on her desk that had been there when she'd arrived. "They're from the men. I still can't believe that I have a husband and five brothers-in-law."

"Don't forget you have a sister-in-law and an aunt too." Georgie leaned back and pointed to the gifts. "You should open them. I've been sent here to make sure that they did well in picking them out. And I think that Zach put the most thought into giving you something."

Emma reached for one of the prettily-wrapped packages and saw who it was from. Jace and Holly, it said. Opening it up, she smiled at the pretty pen and pencil set that had her name engraved on them both.

"I should just let them take these back. I'm pretty sure that when the county finds out about Dirk, I'm going to be fired. And to be honest, I don't blame them one bit. What I did was wrong." Georgie handed her the next box. This one was from Gerard. "Oh, how beautiful."

It was a sun catcher that had a cougar on the bottom of it. She was sure that it could be used as a wind chime as well, but she got up and hung it in the window, and was delighted when she had a rainbow of colors dancing over her desk.

The next gift was from Darin. She sat the large pencil holder on her desk, then smiled when Georgie told her it was a vase. "He made it. There is this pretty girl teaching a pottery class at the local college, and he's taking it. I think that he is enjoying the class more than the girl after he got started. That's his first attempt. I'm very proud of him."

"I love it. I'll have to put some flowers in it when I get home."

Emma took the next box. It was bigger than the rest of them, and she tore the wrapping off. It was from Logan. She looked at Georgie, not sure what it was.

"It's a teat. You know? The things that they hook up to cows to milk them. He wrote a note to go with it. It's that little card. Read it."

To my new sister-in-law. May your tits remain as firm as this one. May your milk run true when you have children, and if you need to, hit Mason with this. It's harder than his head.

She held it to her breast and laughed with Georgie, then set it with the rest of the gifts and picked up the one from Zach. She was almost afraid to open it, but did when Georgie told her it wouldn't hurt her.

Opening it, she thought of all the plans she'd made concerning this office. It had been fun over the last week while waiting on something to happen with her brother. She should have known that it was too good to be true. And when Mason told her she was being silly, she didn't even bother correcting him. But when the watch fell out into the palm of her hand, she looked at Georgie again.

"It was his mother's. She gave it to him the day they left them." Georgie got up and came around the desk to help her put it on. "He came to me last night and told me what he was going to do and why. He's the reason I came by today. To tell you why he did it."

"This should go to his own mate. Someone that he loves." Georgie told him he'd given it to someone he loved. "That's not what I mean. I mean, like his own wife or his own children."

"He wanted you to have it." There was a note to this one as well. She pulled it out of the envelope and started to read it, but her eyes filled with tears and she had to stop. Georgie took it and read it to her.

"'Emma, there are few women that I would call friends in my life. Few of them that I respect. I didn't know my mother well because she died when I was so young, but others in my life have made up for her loss to me. Aunt Georgie because of how much she gave up to come and care for us, and how much she still does just to keep us together. My sister-in-law, Holly, because of her ability to simply be smart and not make you feel like you need a dictionary when you have a conversation with her. But you, you are the one I care for deeply.

"Mason has always been a good man, the best brother, and a wonderful role model. I've wanted to be like him, grow up like him, since I was old enough to realize what he was. Not perfect, but willing to let you know that he was aware of his many flaws and still be a good person. You've made him better.

"He whistles now. Not just a little, but seemingly all the time. Mason smiles now. He did before you came into his life, but there is a twinkle in his eyes now that makes you think that whatever he has, you'll want too. And I do.

"Having a mate has never been a thing that I'd thought of. I'm sure that she's out there…more than likely a human…and she's probably going to give me a run for my money. But I will love her, bring her into my heart, and keep her safe. Because of you.

"Emma, I give you my mother's watch because I simply love you. It was the last thing she ever gave to me, and the only thing in the world that I treasure above all else. One day, when I meet her, the woman that will make me sappy like my brother Jace and happy like my brother Mason, I'd like for you to remind me, should I be stupid, about what I said about love and happiness. Just show me the watch and it will be a reminder that every day is precious to us, and to love with all we have.'

"Then he signed it, 'your loving brother, Zach.'" Emma looked at the watch and wondered, not for the first time since meeting Mason, if his parents would have approved of her. Would they have liked her or just tolerated her? Voicing these questions to Georgie, Emma was surprised when she laughed.

"I was just thinking that maybe they'd think I was…I don't know, a snob. My brother certainly is." Georgie nodded. "Would they have? Liked me I mean?"

"They would have loved you. And been very proud…well, right now they would have been here kicking your ass and wondering why you're not doing your job and telling the rest of the world to fuck off." Emma was shocked by the language and nearly said so. "Norman and Zelma Douglas were the most…everything people I knew. My brother would have told you to get to your job that you're perfect for and don't let anyone bring you down. Zelma, a very strong-willed woman by the way, would have kicked your bottom for sitting here moping too."

Emma heard the phone ring in the outer office and waited for the woman—she thought her name was Celia Holt—to tell her it was for her. When she didn't, Emma looked at Georgie again before speaking.

"Did Mason talk to you?" She nodded and smiled. "I'm really scared, if you want to know the truth. He's been telling me that I'll be fine, that I'm very strong, but I'm still afraid."

"And you should be. It's a scary thing to go from one species to another with someone tearing into your flesh." Emma shivered. "But Mason is strong and so is his cat. If anyone can do it, he'd be the man to do so. Holly had some advantages that you won't. Drugs helped her go through the change with little to no pain on her side. You're going to hurt."

"But he said that it would be over long before I died. I think I'm more afraid of dying and leaving him alone than I am the pain or anything else." Georgie told her she'd do well. "I hope so."

Celia came into her office after a brief knock. "There's a meeting down the hall that they're ready for you to come to now. Sheriff LeBlanc said he'd like for you to be there, but if you're too busy he said to drop everything and get down there anyway."

Emma stood up. It was time. She wondered if she'd have time to come back and get her few things, and decided to stuff them into her purse. She might need them later to cheer her up. Going down the hall, Celia was with her, briefing her on who was going to be in the room with them.

"The sheriff, of course, and then the Ranchers' Association is there as well." Emma looked at Celia and asked her if Mason was there. "Yes, and Jace too. Mr. Snow, as well as Mr. McBride. They're a part of the committee that takes care of things when you're away."

Emma stopped just before the door and turned to Celia. "I'm thinking they're going to fire me. And if they do, I wanted to tell you what an amazing job you've done for me this last week. Whoever they get to replace me...well, they'll need you as much as I did."

"You think they're going to fire you?" Emma nodded. "I don't think so. I had to.... Maybe you should just go in and talk to them. I think you're going to be just fine."

Emma walked just through the doorway and stared. She felt like she was in the wrong room and would have left had Mason not put his arm around her and brought her all the way into the room. There were more people in here than she'd been told, and a good many of them should have been back on their ranches and working.

Balloons were everywhere. The table in the middle of the room was laden with food...cakes and pies, and a ham with loaves of homemade bread that was still steaming, it was so fresh. Her dad and mom were there, standing next to Mr. Snow and Mason's brothers. Emma was handed a plate and told to fill it.

She moved through the line and never saw what was being put on her large tray-like plate. Mason was filling it while people told her congratulations. Nodding, it wasn't until they were both seated at one of the tables that she found her tongue and asked Mason what was going on.

"You're the new mayor." She shook her head. "Yes you are, love. The committee took a vote and it was unanimous. You have the full job instead of just being a fill-in until they find a replacement. Which, I will tell you, it would have been hard to replace you."

"I don't understand." Mason just laughed at her. "Seriously, didn't they read what I wrote about helping my brother out all those times? He was out because of me."

"No, honey, he was out because a judge let him go. You presented the case, which we all got to see by the way, and the judge made his decisions. Both times. And as for him being out because of you, had you not helped us the way you did, he would still be out. You did well and they know it."

The rest of the afternoon was sort of a blur. Emma was presented with a new chair for her office, and some of the other staff, including Celia, were invited in too so they could enjoy the meal and celebrations. Emma was exhausted by the time they got home, and went up to bed early.

~~~

Mason was out in the barn when he heard the bell. It wasn't even noon yet, so he came out quickly and started for the house. The rest of his family was on their way too when the big semi pulled up in front of Georgie's house. She stopped ringing it as soon as they came up on the porch.

"Which one of you did this?" Mason looked at his brothers, then back at Aunt Georgie. "Fess up. I swear to you, I'm only going to get madder if you don't tell me."

"Did what?" She glared at him, and he took a step back. "You know what's in the truck? If you do then if you told us, maybe we can tell you something about it."

"You don't know." He shook his head and watched as the rest of them did the same. "Well, this is just dandy. I have a delivery here and not one person ordered it for me. I guess I'll have to send it—"

The car stopping in the drive sprayed rocks and dirt up over the porch. When Emma and Holly got out, Mason had an idea who might have ordered whatever had his aunt all twisted up. Aunt Georgie glared at them when Emma walked up to the driver and told him to unload it.

"I'm not going to accept this." The driver ignored her, as did Emma and Holly. "You heard me. I said I don't want it."

"Yes, you do." Holly helped the driver pull the last of the plastic off the back end before she came up to kiss Aunt Georgie too. "Now, behave yourself and say thank you."

The driver, using a lift off the back end of his truck, brought down the first box. It was huge and the only writing on it said "fragile" and "this end up." When he went back up to get the next load, Mason and his brothers moved the box up onto the porch. The sucker was heavy too.

Cutting into the tape that held the box together, Mason stepped back when he realized what was inside. It was a chair. One that his aunt had wanted since…well, since forever.

The next few boxes were a couch, loveseat, and lamps. All of it matched the chair, and each piece made his aunt cry harder. When they had wrestled all the old out and the new in, he realized how worn out and used up the furniture was. It also suddenly dawned on him that they'd been avoiding the living room, a room that they had gathered in after every meal. Now they stayed in the dining room, or on the porch if the weather was nice.

In addition to the living room furniture, there was a kitchen table and chairs, a stove, appliances that nearly filled all the space on the counters, and a huge mixer, coffee maker, and tea maker. There was a new can opener, electric, that was being hung under the cabinets by Gerard as the rest of the boxes were opened. Mason went to find his wife to thank her and to ask her how she knew.

"Last week Holly and I were here helping her get dinner ready. It was as if she was living in the Dark Ages. Did you know that she was mixing things with a nineteen thirties hand mixer? Anyway, we saw that she was in desperate need of an overhaul. So we took her to town with us and did some window shopping with her. It was a blast." Mason kissed her on the nose and told her how much he loved her. "I know, and I'm that awesome."

He was tickling her when Aunt Georgie came into the room. She had been crying again, something that Mason only just realized he'd not seen her do much of. Instead of leaving her to Emma as she asked him to do, he called for the family and waited for them to come in.

"We've been horrible nephews." When Aunt Georgie started to protest, he stopped her. "We have. We should have seen what you had to work with and done more to help you out. You've taken such good care of us and now...now, thanks to Emma and Holly, you're going to be working less hard and having more time for the grandchildren, because let's face it, a grandmother is just what you're going to be to our kids."

"I don't know what to say." Aunt Georgie hugged them all and held onto Holly and Emma while she looked at all of them. "I will say this. If one of you comes into my house now and doesn't wipe your feet, or tries to put your feet up on the furniture or anything else to ruin my new things, I'm going to box your ears."

"How did you know to be upset when the truck came into the yard?" Mason had wondered that too, and was glad that Logan had asked. It was like she knew what was in the big thing. "You were really ticked off and I, for one, was really glad that I had nothing to do with it when you stood there looking like the wrath of the devil."

"I got a call. From the shipping company. And I asked him what was in the load, thinking that it would either go to the barn or Jace and Holly's house. When he told me it was living room furniture and that it was for Georgina Douglas, I just knew what it was." She looked at Emma and Holly. "I never dreamed you two would have outwitted the boys. But now that I think on it, I should have known it was you from the start."

Dinner that night was a strange affair. There was Chinese food and pizza, tacos and steak, and when Palmer came with donuts and pie and a gift for the "new" house, they weren't surprised when Landon and Katie showed up with ice cream and a gift as well. They were a family, blended and bonded. After dinner, Landon asked to speak to Mason.

"I got a call from the jail this morning." Landon had told him yesterday that while he knew his son was in prison, the term "jail" was easier for him and Katie to deal with. "They said that Dirk wants to see me. He wants his mom too, but she told me she's just not ready to go and see him just yet. Not that she hates him, but…well, she's hurting."

So was Landon. He'd aged over the last several days, and Mason would bet that he wasn't sleeping well either.

The man was in a great deal of pain, and there was little to nothing anyone could do about it.

"Do you want me to go with you?" Landon looked so relieved that he had to smile. "You can ask me anything you like, Landon. Anything. I've told you that before. Just tell me when you want to go and I'll be there. Just give me enough time to make sure that there is help for the milkers."

"I was thinking in the morning. Can you do that?" Mason nodded, realigning his day mentally to help the man out. "I just want to get it over with. Emma, she wanted to go too, but well, I just want to do this myself. I know that you're going, but you're there to help me pick up the pieces should it go as badly as I think it will."

"He's not where he can hurt anyone anymore. You know that." Landon nodded and looked out over the field. "I wanted to talk to you anyway. Emma wants me to convert her to a cougar. She wants me to do it soon, before we have any children."

"That's my girl. Will she be able to…? I don't know how all this works, son. Tell me what you're going to do." Mason only gave him the highlights. Not the details because, frankly, they scared him a little too much to dwell on. "She'll be fine then?"

"I believe so. It's not a long process to start, but she might be down for a few days. Just until her body adjusts. Rest is what she'll have, and I won't leave her during that time."

"Of course you won't. I'd expect no less of you. I'll see to the ranch while you're held up with her. And so you know, me and my Katie, we moved back home. Next month she and I are going to go on an extended vacation, our first in nearly forty years."

Landon told him all the spots they were going to go. France, Scotland, Germany. They were even planning to go to some of the islands....a cruise was going to start them off. Then they'd end it on a train coming back across the United States, stopping wherever the train did. He looked excited and ready to go now.

They set up to meet at his house at six in the morning. Mason had already talked to Jace and Logan, and they were going to cover for him for the early milking. The hands on his ranch, the McBride ranch, were already moving to care for the moving of the steer to help out the Double Deuce for breeding purposes. The day was set and all he had to do was tell Emma what he was going to do. He hoped that she'd not want to go in a way, but wanted her there in the event that things went badly. He went to find her after talking to Landon.

The men of the house were loading dishes in the new dishwasher as he entered the kitchen. The women had been retired to the living room, so he knew that he'd have a few minutes to let them all know what was going to happen in the morning, including the visit with Dirk.

"You think he'll say something stupid?" Mason just looked at Darin. "Yeah, stupid question. When has he not said something stupid? Christ, the things he's done to his own family boggles the mind."

"No kidding." Jace handed Mason a dish towel as he continued. "I'll take care of the day for you if you promise to take Landon for a few beers afterwards. He's going to need it, and we won't worry about him driving home after if you're driving."

Mason helped finish up the kitchen with them and Palmer, and Jace went to the office to work on some upcoming issues that were about to come up with the new mill. Gerard had already agreed to run it so long as he got to hire who he wanted to help out. Neither, so far as Mason knew, had a problem with that.

By midnight, they were home. It was their first night in the house alone since they'd moved in, and Mason was excited. Apparently so was Emma. She met him at the bedroom door naked and smelling like pure sex. Mason let his cat take him so he could have some fun with her too.

CHAPTER 14

Dirk sat in his room and watched the clock roll around to the hour. He'd been told he had visitors, but he couldn't see them until ten o'clock. As soon as he was out of here, he was going to sue this place and then burn it to the ground. The nerve of these people thinking that he should have to follow rules like the rest of them did. And he was clearly not like the rest of the people that inhabited this place.

At ten he stood up, no small feat considering that he had chains on his ankles and wrists; another thing he was going to have his dad take care of was his living conditions. If he had to stay here, he should be treated the way that his station demanded. This…this treating him like an animal wasn't a McBride way to be treated.

He was led to a room that held a single table and three chairs. Dirk was shoved into the only one on his side of the table and told to put his hands on top. He knew better than to argue with this man. He'd hit him yesterday when he'd told him no. Putting his hands up, the chains were put in the large ring in the middle of the table, and then his legs were shackled to the loops on the floor.

"You do know that this is my father coming and he's going to set me free." The man, Bull his nametag said, just ignored him as he stood near the table. "You're all going to be out of work when he sees what you've done to me."

The door behind him opened and Dirk didn't even bother turning. He knew who it was and wasn't all that thrilled to see him. But he wanted out of here, and if his dad was the only way to get out, then so be it. But when Mason sat down with his dad, Dirk tried to go after him. A big hand on his shoulder held him down along with the chains.

"I do not want to see that piece of shit." Mason only smiled and his dad paled. "Dad, this is between the two of us. And since Mason is the reason I'm in here, I'd rather you just send him back to the ranch to work."

"He's my son-in-law, Dirk, and whatever you have to say to me, you can say to him." Dirk snarled. He was sick to death of being told no. "What did you want?"

"What do I want? Can't you see where the fuck I'm at? I want you to pay these people off and get me the fuck out of here. These people are crazy, and I'm not going to let you put me away as if you wish to forget me." He leaned back in the chair and tried to organize his thoughts. There were so many in his head lately that he hurt from it. "They beat me. And I have to be treated like an animal. This is not right for a McBride, a man like me, to be treated. Do whatever it takes for me to come home, and I'll pretend that you didn't have me put away."

"I had not a thing to do with you being put in here. You did that all on your own when you killed those people. If you let these people help you, perhaps you can lead a productive life here and do something with yourself."

"I'm not staying here." His dad looked at Mason. "Did he put you up to this? I'm betting he did. I'm Dirk McBride, doesn't that mean a damned thing to any of you? Christ, this is the stupidest thing. And let me tell you, you have done some really stupid things, but this is by far the worst. Let me the fuck out of here. I don't care how much of my money you have to use, just do it."

"You really do expect him to just do this for you, don't you?" Dirk nodded, not really wanting to talk to Mason, but if it got his dad to get moving, then so be it. "You just expect that because you want something that it should be yours at whatever harm it would cause someone else."

"Of course I should have what I want. I don't see why that should be a problem to get it either. The money is right there. It's not like he's going to live long enough to use it. Christ, didn't you know that cancer is eating him alive? And when he goes, it'll all be mine anyway. Just get with the program and get me out of here." Mason shook his head. "What is it with you? Don't you know who I am? What kind of influence my money will have over everyone, including you? You're nothing to me."

"You got that right. I'm not a thing to you. And as for your dad, he doesn't have cancer any longer. The doctor thinks that he'll live another thirty or forty years the way his health is. I don't think you're going to make it that long, and you're not getting a dime of his money."

Dirk jerked on the chains and screamed. He was fucking sick of this.

"Dad, I'm not going to tell you again to Get. Me. The. Fuck. Out. Of. Here." When his dad stood up, Dirk looked at Mason. "See what I am to him? His son, and he'll do whatever I tell him, because I'm Dirk McBride."

His dad went to the door, and Dirk was already making plans to go to the mall. There were so many things he'd need now. Shirts and sweaters, pants, as well as all new underthings. This place had taken away all his silk and left him with only cotton. When his dad told him good-bye, Dirk frowned.

"I'm not coming back here. And I'm going to leave a message at the desk for you not to be able to call me again. I don't...I never raised you to be like this, and I won't have you hurting me or my family again."

Dirk started to speak but looked at Mason when he laughed.

"You're doing this. I won't have it. You're nothing. Do you hear me? Nothing. And when I get out of here, and I will, you're going to pay for what you're doing to me. I'm Dirk McBride. No one treats me this way. No one." Dirk watched them both go out the door. "Dad, get back here. I want you to get me out of here. I'm not going to let you treat me this way and get away with it. Get me out of here now!"

Bull helped him to stand, and Dirk decided that he'd had enough. Jerking from him, he tried to get to the door and out when his head was slammed against the wall. Dirk fell hard and knew that he was going to need medical attention as soon as he got out of here. Standing again, his feet got tangled in the chains and he pitched forward.

~~~

Landon wasn't sure what he should be feeling. He was ashamed to admit that he was somewhat relieved that it was over. But he had a guilt that just wouldn't let go, and he wasn't sure it was because of what had happened or the fact that he was just glad.

Just as they were leaving, two guards had been standing at the entrance of the place and had asked them to come back inside. Mason had turned his truck around and had parked in the place where they'd directed them.

Getting out, they were asked to please go inside but not to go to the desk. Someone would come and get them.

Landon had wanted to ask, desperately wanted to know if his son had convinced someone to let him go and they were going to have to take him back. He was terrified of what he might do if they knew that he didn't want him. Not in his home and certainly not in his life. But when a police cruiser pulled up in front of the building, Landon staggered.

"I got you." Mason had helped him to a seat. Landon's knees had been so wobbly that he felt had he not held him, he would have most assuredly landed on his ass. As it was, he was still shaky and his head was pounding.

They were still sitting there an hour later when the administrator and two officers came to get them. Mason helped him up, but he was now able to stand on his own. Landon was ready to beg them to keep Dirk when they were escorted to an office.

"There's been an accident." Again he staggered, but there had been a chair behind him this time as he fell back. "I'm sorry. We've been going over the video several times, and we don't know how it happened."

"Perhaps if you just tell us what you're talking about, we'll be able to keep up." The woman, Delia Angle, nodded and asked Mason to have a seat. "If it's all the same to you, I'd rather stand. And since I know that none of you are human, I'd like to tell you that my cat is getting really pissy. So if you don't mind, just fucking get on with it. Has Dirk convinced you to let him go?"

"No. I'm so sorry to tell you like this, but he's dead." Landon sat there and had tried twice to ask her if she was joking, or at least ask her how it had happened. But he had been speechless. And now they were headed home.

"I'm not sure what to ask you. Did you...? I'm not sure." Mason said he understood and was there for him. "He's gone. I mean...did they tell us what happened?"

"Yes. He was trying to break free of the guard when he hit the wall pretty hard. His face was bloodied and bruised pretty badly. When he stood up again, the guard, his name is Bull, reached for him to bring him back to the table when Dirk tried to run again. This time his legs were tangled up in the restraints and he fell forward. Bull told us that he hit his temple on the edge of the table and was dead even before he hit the floor."

"He didn't suffer then?" Mason told him it didn't look like it. "They showed us the tape. I remember that now. It was...he was mad to get away from the guard and I saw that he...he's dead, Mason. I know he was a bad person, but he was my son."

"I'm so sorry, Landon. I don't know what it would be like to lose someone like this." Landon was pretty sure that Mason knew just how it felt but said nothing. The boy had lost his parents at some point in his life. "I've told Emma. She's going to tell her mom if you want her to."

"Yes. I think...I'm not sure what I'd say to her right now. I'm just...I have no idea, to be honest with you. And I feel guilty too, if you want to know the truth." Mason only nodded. "I'm a horrible person, aren't I?"

"No. You're a good man who was dealt a hard blow. Not just with the death of your son, even though that was tragic enough, but you're dealing with all the things he left behind for you to take care of too. I'd like to admit that I'm somewhat glad that it happened this way. A long trial would have been too much on Katie and you." Landon nodded and looked out the window. "Emma said to tell you that she loves you so much, and that she's helping Katie."

"Katie is all I ever wanted in the world when we first met." Talking about his wife was easier than talking about his son. "She was the most beautiful woman I'd ever seen then, and still is to this day. Katie had this way about her that was both calming and had me all twisted up in knots all the time. And asking her to marry me about did me in."

"Emma looks like her. And I'm betting when she gets older, she'll be just as beautiful." Landon nodded. He was a very lucky man to have Mason as a son-in-law. "We've been talking while I've been driving, and we were wondering if you two might come and stay with us in the house when you get back. You don't have to make it forever if you don't like it, but we'd love to have you there."

"I lived there as a boy. I could tell you things about that house that would curl your toes." He leaned back and smiled at the memories. "My mom, she had the house when she married my father. He was a good man, stern but fair. I wanted to be like him since the first time I saw him dealing with a thief on our land. The man had stolen a steer and was butchering it."

"He was hungry." Landon nodded. "Katie told me about him. His family was your foreman's ancestors. That's why they've been in the family helping you all these years. I think it's a wonderful story."

"It is. It is at that." Landon thought of his son. "I guess I'll have to make some arrangements to get him buried and all. I was just thinking that under the circumstances that we should just have a quiet family thing."

"Emma is arranging to have his body shipped to your funeral home. They'll do an autopsy and all, but that shouldn't be too long." Landon nodded. "And she's called in a few favors at the paper to have nothing put in the paper until after the funeral, whenever you decide to have it."

Landon nodded. He was simply overwhelmed. And he wanted to hold his Katie. She was taking this hard, he knew that. And as much as he wanted to sob on her shoulder, he was going to hold onto her while she grieved. Landon was still having problems figuring out what he was feeling. All he could put a finger on right now was that his son was gone.

His Katie was waiting for him on the front porch of Mason's home. When he got out of the truck, he moved to her like a man in a trance. She took him into her arms and they both just stood there, neither of them crying or speaking, just holding onto each other for now. When she spoke—his Katie always knew what to say—he looked at her.

"People always say when something like this happens that the person is in a better place. I don't think that's what is going on this time. I think…as much as I hate to admit this, I think we're the ones in a better place because of his passing." Landon nodded, his heart twisting in his chest at the truth of her words. "Dirk had been…he'd been pushing us away most of his life. Hurting us in one way or another. And now…now he's gone away, and we're here to pick up our own lives."

Landon felt better knowing that she was feeling the same way. "He was so angry with me when I was leaving him. Spewing stuff at me like I was nothing to him. Less than nothing really. If that had been my father and me talking to him like that, I'd have been picking my head up for the next month."

"Emma said that he didn't suffer. Did he?" Landon told her no, not at all. "That day he hurt you, nearly killed you, I decided that I was done with him. I hate to admit it, and I will only to you, but I'm glad that it's done. A long trial and all that went with it would have hurt all of us, including the Douglas family and Palmer."

He told her what Mason had said about moving in with them for a time. She agreed it might not be so bad. "I don't think I'd want to go back to the house just yet. There are so many things there that would remind us of Dirk."

And not any of them good memories. Landon was finally at peace with what had happened. That wasn't to say in a few weeks he wouldn't think about Dirk and hurt some, but for now, with his feelings validated somewhat by Katie, he was better. Going into the house, they caught sight of Emma and Mason on the deck behind the house and stood watching them.

"He's going to convert her to a cat soon." Katie nodded. "She'll be his match in all things, he told me. The leader of his leap, small as it is, but she'll be a leader too."

"She'll be very good at it, I think. Strong as she is, their children are going to be so much fun to see." Landon couldn't wait to hold a grandchild in his arms. "Emma said that she and Mason were going to try when things settle around the ranches. Did you know that he and the other ranchers are going together to buy up the Mitchell ranch? Seems Gordon has run into some financial issues. His wife caught him with his young secretary, and she's taking him to the cleaners."

"Man should learn where to keep his dick." Katie smacked him on the arm and told him to behave. Before he could tell her he was, they watched as Mason went from a man standing there to a big cougar in a single heartbeat. "Holy shit."

Mason moved to Emma and rubbed his head on her legs. When she took off running to the woods, Mason turned and looked at the two of them. Landon felt like a deer in the headlights. As soon as Mason yawned, showing off the biggest teeth he'd ever seen, Mason took off to the woods too. Landon looked at Katie.

"She'll be fine." He nodded at his wife. "More than fine. He won't ever let anything or anyone hurt her again."

Before You Go…

Share your voice and help guide other readers to these wonderful books. Even if it's only a line or two your reviews help readers discover the author's books so they can continue creating stories that you'll love. Login to your favorite retailer and leave a review. Thank you.

AWARD WINNING, BESTSELLING AUTHOR

Kathi Barton, author of the bestselling series Force of Nature, lives in Nashport, Ohio with her husband Paul. In addition to writing full time Kathi likes to spend time with her eight grandkids, three children and three children-in-laws. She writes to relax and have fun.

Her muse, a cross between Jimmy Stewart and Hugh Jackman brings them to life for her readers in a way that has them coming back time and again for more. Her favorite genre is paranormal romance with a great deal of spice. You can visit Kathi on line and drop her an email if you'd like. She loves hearing from her fans. aaronskiss@gmail.com.

Follow Kathi on her blog:
http://kathisbartonauthor.blogspot.com/